sto ✓

GREEDY
MARIANI

For Rob and Terry

Contents

CONTENTS

GREEDY
MARIANI

TALES OF
HOW AND WHY

How the Moonfish
Came to Be

In ancient times the Sun was married to the Moon. And the Moon, like a beautiful medallion, hung in the sky, shining night and day.

The sun hung there, too, but he did his shining in the daytime. He was not lazy exactly—but he believed work (in this case, shining) should take place only from sunup until sundown. And very strict about his hours he was, too.

Not so the Moon. Day and night she gleamed away. But perhaps the Sun was right. All work and no play. . . . At any rate the Moon grew bored. And one evening it took her fancy to make a journey to earth. She let herself fall—*bime!* right on an island. Then like a hoop she rolled to the beach. There she regarded the sea.

That night the sea was smooth, as a great sheet of zinc. However, from time to time little waves came rippling to the foot of the cocoa trees. The Moon began to play with them. She skipped. She skipped again. Then, *floupe!* she jumped onto the sea.

Over the waves she tripped. Over the waves she hopped. She raced the waves to the scalloped shore. And back again. She came, she went, she returned, she danced. And so she played the night through. Ah, it was lovely. Much better than hanging like a chandelier, so quiet, so lofty, high in the sky.

In the morning Moon slid under the waves. The water was clear; it was warm. Fish of all colors and shapes moved without sound. A rosy glow bathed the depths of the sea. The Moon saw thickets of coral, a galaxy of starfish, a rainbow of sponges, fish without eyes. She saw a white tortoise whose shell was of silver encrusted with gold and gems.

The fish were astonished. Imagine a golden saucer of a moon skimming through the sea. They had never seen anything like it.

On earth the people were even more astounded. Perplexed, too. What had happened to Moon? Everyone went and hid himself in his cottage. All feared a work of the Devil.

4

All this time le Bon Dieu (which is another name for God) was watching. Le Bon Dieu has patience. Oh, yes, and to spare. But at the end of hours and hours He grew angry. (By then even His spare patience was giving out.)

"Return to the sky, Moon," He commanded.

But the Moon paid Him no heed. Foolish Moon!

"Fetch me the Moon," demanded le Bon Dieu of all the dwellers of the earth, the sea and the air. "She is in the Caribbean Sea," He added.

Evening arrived according to custom. Moon climbed to the top of the sea to dance. Immediately the stars overhead sank down, down until they rested on a lacy cloud. And all the fireflies of the Antilles swarmed about Moon.

Moon, full of joy, thought they had come to dance a quadrille with her. They would have a party, a ball!

She was quickly undeceived. The fishermen tumbled into their boats. Horns sounded the summons. For who was willing to disobey le Bon Dieu? (Besides Moon, that is.) Canoes, skiffs, rafts, dinghies, sailboats, rowboats, yawls, sculls took to the water. They advanced in the glimmer of torches.

The fishers approached the Moon, singing in chorus,

> *"Seize, seize, seize the Moon! Oh! Oh! Oh!*
> *Seize, seize, seize the Moon! Oh! Oh! Oh!"*

And the chant reverberated between the bluffs.

The Moon sensed danger. She wished to slip under the water. But underneath the sea the sharks, the eels, the sea serpents all together formed an impassable net.

Then Mother Beak, the mother of all herons, tore Moon with her long bill. The sawfish jabbed with his jagged teeth. The squid threatened her with snaky arms. The sea urchins unsheathed their prickles and loosened them in the bruised body of the Moon. Poor Moon. She was ripped and ragged from her wounds. On top of the water Moon wavered and trembled.

Still the chant went on,

> *"Seize, seize, seize the Moon! Oh! Oh! Oh!*
> *Seize, seize, seize the Moon! Oh! Oh! Oh!"*

At last the Moon was encircled by the chant and the fishermen, their torches in their hands. They picked up the Moon. She was a prisoner. They brought her before le Bon Dieu (who was still very angry).

Le Bon Dieu spoke. "My daughter, all mischief deserves chastisement. I fastened you in the sky. I told you to be beautiful and not to stir. You disobeyed me. You were a pretty damsel, round as a grapefruit, and now you are chipped and torn."

Moon hung her head.

Le Bon Dieu took her in His hands. He pulled off the shreds and tatters. He molded her back into her former shape. Only now she was smaller, more like an orange.

6

"So much for you," said le Bon Dieu. "You will have to remain so. I shall suspend you again in the sky, for there you belong. As punishment I will separate you from your husband the Sun. When he arises you will lie down. The moment you get up he will come to rest. You will not see him again, little vagabond. And you will never have children. Thus you will live eternally."

Le Bon Dieu frowned in a troubled way. "Still, slipping through the water as you did, Moon, you were beautiful. Yes . . . very nice. But I cannot turn you loose in the sea again. My creatures must not waste their time playing tag with you. And yet, yet . . ."

Le Bon Dieu, pondering deeply, dropped the leftover fragments of Moon into the sea. He crumbled them into dust and threw them over the swells. From that time on, the Caribbean Sea has been phosphorescent. All for a moonish prank.

Then le Bon Dieu took clay. He kneaded it, He rolled it, He flattened it. From it He made a round moon—golden yellow. He made two eyes, a mouth, two fins, a tail. He breathed on it and said, "You shall be the moon of the water and you shall have many children."

With a flip of his tail the moonfish squirmed in le Bon Dieu's hands. Since that time the moonfish swims in the sea of the Antilles, in company with butterfly fish, squirrelfish, flying fish and many others.

And when they sell fish the fishers cry,

> *"Here are the flying fish,*
> *Here the striped burrfish,*
> *The fish angel Gabriel,*
> *The moonfish. . . .*
> *But the full moon still hangs high in the sky."*

And le Bon Dieu laughs. He is happy to see there are plenty of moonfish to fill the Caribbean, where they flash like gold coins in the green sea.

From the Antilles
Georgel, Thérèse. *Contes et Légendes des Antilles*

How the Clever Doctor
Tricked Death

There was once a very rough fellow who always had a fine idea trickling through his head: once I find work I am sure to become rich quickly. He had faith. The desire to search for work he had not.

One day Death stood before him. "Fellow, I have taken a fancy to you. Such a strong fancy that I will look out for you. Now heed me. You shall take the profession of doctor. As *médico* you will be able to cure anyone on whom you lay your hand—on these conditions. If you see me standing at the foot of the sick one's bed you may cure him at once. But, if you see me at the *head* of the bed, do not trouble yourself. Go for a walk. Play some chess. Sip a cup of coffee. There is no cure, and he is mine."

The fellow went off to the city and began to practice medicine. *His* type of medicine. Not a bad type either. After a time he had cured dozens—hundreds—thousands of patients. Soon there ran through the town a rumor that a doctor lived therein who could accomplish miracles. The rumor, after many twists and turns and rushing into blind alleys, finally reached the palace. Here it was welcomed by the King, who had a daughter, gravely ill. At once he sent for the doctor.

As soon as this one arrived breathless (one doesn't skimp on breath at a king's summons), the King spoke. "The princess is ill. Seriously ill. If you save her you shall have half my kingdom. And marry the princess in the bargain. On the other hand, if you allow her to die— off comes your head."

Rather unfair of the King. He gave the doctor no choice at all. So you can imagine what choice the doctor *did* make. He agreed. Oh, heartily. Anyway, he was convinced he could cure the girl. No problem. He was so accustomed to seeing Death at the foot of the bed, the old rascal might have been a bedpost.

But *this* time—lo and behold, Death stood big as life at the *head* of the bed. It gave the doctor quite a turn. Ay, he said to himself, instead of curing her and living like a

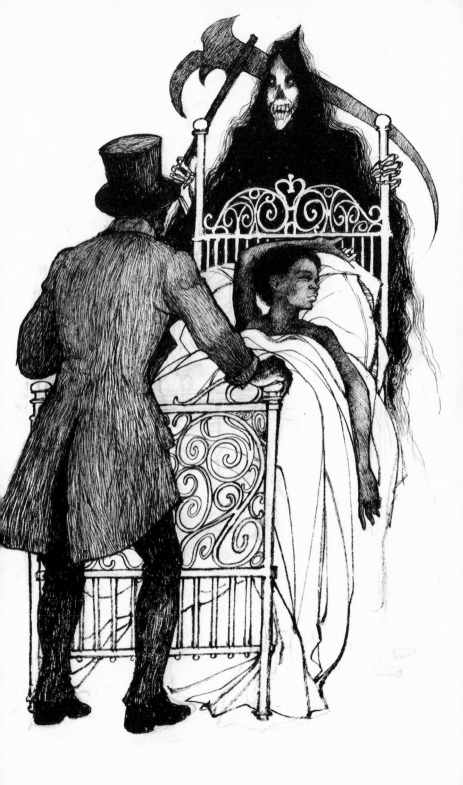

king, am I to die? Are we both to die? *Ay,* what to do? *Ay, ay, ay.* . . .

Then an idea came. Swiftly he seized the bed and yanked it around foot to wall instead of head to wall. And Death suddenly found himself at the foot of the bed—watching the doctor assist the cured princess to sit up. Wasn't he put out! Furious. He sallied out the door swearing revenge on the clever doctor.

At least the King kept his promise. (They sometimes don't, you know.) He made the arrangement for handing over half his riches and also set the date for the wedding. After all, it's rather nice to have a doctor in the family, particularly a good one.

However, when the doctor left the palace, who should catch his sleeve but—Death. "Come with me," he commanded.

Before he knew it the doctor was up in the sky, standing on a heavenly blue carpet. And around him were hundreds—thousands—millions of little oil lamps.

"See you these lamps?" asked Death sternly. "Each one is the life of someone on earth. When the oil is gone so is the life. Here is yours—this with only a dab of wetness in the bottom. Five minutes of flame. Five minutes of life, my clever doctor."

"Very well." The doctor sighed. "But add enough oil to last fifteen minutes and I shall tell you a story. One of my best. . . ."

How the Clever Doctor Tricked Death

He watched to see where Death dipped out a centigram of oil. Then while he told his story, though it was a good one, Death dozed, and the doctor refueled his lamp . . . to the very top and dribbling over. So that even today he still lives. I know, for he is an old acquaintance of mine. He it is who told me this tale.

From the Dominican Republic
Andrade, Manuel J. *Folklore de la República Dominicana*

Why Dog
Lost His Voice

One day God descended to earth to inspect the efforts of man. Day after day He traveled about, examining the work of the farmers and taking note of their activity or their idleness.

Each morning He passed the same group and greeted them, *"Messieurs,* how are you today?" (No one knew that this was God.)

They answered, "We strive to live."

"When do you expect to finish weeding?"

"Tomorrow, before evening."

God saluted them, wished them good luck and went on His way, accompanied by His companion, Dog. At that time the dog was wise and understood many things. He even spoke man's tongue. Better than man did. A clever creature, Dog.

The next day at dawn the peasants found that the portion of the field they had weeded the day before was again snarled with vines and thickets. They set their hands to work, grumbling about the enthusiasm of weeds.

Just then God and Dog sauntered by and spoke to the farmers as usual. "Good morning, *messieurs,* and how goes it?"

"We struggle still."

"And the field—when will it be cleared?"

"Tomorrow, perhaps, before nightfall."

The Traveler bowed and continued on His way. Next day the field was more tangled than ever. And this state of affairs lasted a long time—a long, long time. The farmers became more and more discouraged. The more they weeded, the faster grew the weeds. The more God greeted them, the sulkier *they* grew.

One day when the midday sun shone so fierily as to burn one's throat, God said to Dog, "I am thirsty. Go to those laborers and bring me back a drink."

Dog went off running and, having obtained water from the workers, he whispered to them, "Sirs, after this when you answer the questions of that old fellow I am with, always reply with, 'Good morning, gracious Papa God!' or 'By the grace of God.' You will see this is fine advice."

The following morning God passed the farmers. For once they spoke first. "Good morning, gracious Papa God."

God turned a stern eye on Dog, who hung his head. Then He asked the men, "Eh, my children, when do you think to complete this work?"

"This afternoon, by the grace of God."

Scarcely had these words been spoken than the field was free of all useless growth. Clear as a plate. God marched away, followed by Dog, who with lowered head glanced to right and left, anywhere but at God.

16

His master reproached him for his conduct and said, "You have betrayed me and must be punished."

Since then, Dog has depended on man rather than the other way around, which God had first intended. Dog also lost the use of speech and could make no sound but a mere bark. Perhaps that is just as well. One could wish for less chatter in the world rather than more.

From Haiti
Bastien, Rémy. *Anthologie du Folklore Haitien*

Why Misery Remains in the World

Well, *amigos,* there was this old woman, very old, who lived alone in her hut. No more company had she than a pretty pear tree that grew at the door.

The boys of the neighborhood—the *vecindad*—called her crazy and treated her badly. Not surprising—boys being what they are. Whenever pears appeared on the pear tree these *malcriados,* those "badly brought up ones," came to tease the poor old woman and steal away her fruit.

One day a pilgrim stopped at the door of the hut. "Good woman, may I lay my head on your stick of firewood for the night?"

Aunt Misery, as the boys and neighbors all called her, invited him in. The pilgrim entered, supped and spent the night there (with a softer pillow than a stick).

The next morning as he was leaving he spoke. "Ask what you will, *vieja,* old one. Whatsoever you wish, it will be granted you."

"I desire only one thing."

"And that is?"

"I wish that anyone who climbs my pear tree will be unable to come down until I permit it."

"You shall have your wish."

So it was when next the pear tree bore fruit the boys arrived on the scene, screaming ungentle names, and prepared to carry off all the fruit they could. They even brought buckets and baskets. They planned a complete harvest. It did not quite work out that way.

The moment they were in the tree they found themselves as glued to the branches as the pears themselves. More so. For the pears could be plucked, but the boys could not. There they sat, stuck fast.

The names they called Aunt Misery changed from ungracious to gracious. And the things they promised her—fresh fish everyday, a hen, two hens, a rooster, chickens enough to cover a square kilometer! They pleaded so hard with Aunt Misery that at the end she consented to free them on the condition that never again would they return to molest her. *Never.*

They couldn't wait to promise—and meant it, too. Before, they had only *thought* her a witch; now they *knew*.

Some time went by. A pleasant time for Aunt Misery—left in peace to enjoy her pears.

One afternoon there presented himself at the door another traveler, one who appeared somewhat flurried. Not relaxed at all. When Aunt Misery saw him she asked what he wished.

"I am Death, and I have come for you."

Aunt Misery, placid as a still pool, responded, "Very well. But before leaving, I wish to pick some pears. Will you be so good as to help me?"

Grumbling under his breath, Death climbed the pear tree, shook the branches, lowered a foot to climb down—and quickly drew it back. There he crouched, helpless as a fly tangled in a spiderweb. For Aunt Misery was in no mood to permit him to leave. Old she might be—but still lively as a grasshopper.

Years passed. No one died. Everyone grew older and older and there was no end to it. Murmurs and complaints were heard from doctors, druggists, undertakers and priests, who were all going out of business. Even some of the elderly began to protest. "We are tired," they whined. "We wish to start afresh in the next world."

Aunt Misery was not one of these. The world, sad as it was, suited her splendidly. So she made a pact with

Death. She would free him if he would spare her. Thus it is that as long as the world is the world, Misery will never die.

From Puerto Rico
Ramírez de Arellano, Rafael. *Folklore Portorriqueño*

How El Bizarrón
Fooled the Devil

There was once a man called El Bizarrón who wandered about looking for work. A restless fellow. He wandered here. He wandered there. But more often there than here.

One day he was told that in the house of the Devil there was need for a servant. *"Pues, ten cuidado!"* they warned. (A forceful way of saying, "Watch out!") Two servants the Devil had already slain. He was a mean one. All who worked for him ended up dead. Much sooner than later, too. Clearly a recommendation to avoid *that* house.

But El Bizarrón retorted, "I'm on my way. The Devil won't frighten *me*."

So, to the Devil's front door he went. And knocked. Who should open the door but the Devil himself.

"Have you work for a strong man?"

"Work enough for six strong men. You are sure there are not five more of you? Ah, well. *Pase adentro*."

In walked El Bizarrón. The Devil led him to the room where he was to sleep. "Rest," he said. "Tomorrow you will begin your chores."

El Bizarrón stretched himself on the bed. Before long, healthy snores were livening up that corner of the house.

The next day the Devil sent him to fetch water.

But El Bizarrón demanded, "Give me a pick and shovel."

The Devil without any fuss gave them.

El Bizarrón went down to the river. He began digging a ditch from the stream to the Devil's house. Like six men he toiled. Well . . . like three anyway.

At eleven o'clock came the Devil to check up on El Bizarrón. "Water I wish. Not a ditch. Explain yourself," he commanded.

"I am digging a canal to your house. Then there will be no need to go for water. Water will flow to you."

The Devil reflected. This man can dig. The trench is already the depth of a pitchfork. (The Devil knew his pitchforks.) Moreover, this man can *think*. He didn't like that at all. It was such a distasteful thought that he went off home.

A few days later the Devil ordered El Bizarrón to fetch a load of wood. El Bizarrón demanded, "Give me a length of rope. A long length."

Without much ado the Devil gave it.

El Bizarrón took the rope on his shoulder and went off to the mountain. There he set himself to wind the rope around the trees—around the whole forest. The rope was a lengthy length all right. With all his tramping, the heels of El Bizarrón's shoes were worn to a fraction of a millimeter; not enough sole remained to measure a fraction of anything. At eleven o'clock when the Devil came to see what El Bizarrón was up to, he found him with the rope looped around the mountain as a collar wreathes a neck.

Of course he wanted to know, "What are you doing?"

El Bizarrón answered, "Securing this mountain of woods so I can carry it back in one trip."

What a barbarian, thought the Devil. And he directed El Bizarrón to return to the house. Without the mountain. No room for *that* in the backyard.

Soon after, there was a throwing contest on the beach, with metal bars. The Devil thought, ah, I shall send this strong fellow as a competitor. With his muscles he must surely win me a prize. And he led El Bizarrón to the shore, El Bizarrón with a bar balanced on his shoulder.

At the beach everyone was practicing and preparing himself for the match. Except El Bizarrón. That one curled himself on the sunny sand and took a snooze.

The day peeled off its hours. The contest began. Came the turn of El Bizarrón.

Loudly he cried out, "Order those faraway boats to sail away. Otherwise I will sink them with my shot!"

As this was impossible they would not permit him to throw. It was a disappointment to all. In particular to the Devil, who felt more and more uneasy about El Bizarrón's strength. *And* his acuteness. Too dangerous is this ox with his fox's brain, he decided. I must rid myself of him.

The two made their way back to the Devil's house. In a buttery manner the Devil suggested that since he desired to spend that night stretched out on the iron grill of the barbecue, El Bizarrón might wish to sleep beneath.

"Why not?" asked El Bizarrón in an offhand way.

So it was arranged. The Devil then hid two heavy, heavy rocks that he planned to drop on El Bizarrón during the night.

Evening fell, and both lay down in their places: the Devil on the high grill and El Bizarrón underneath. But El Bizarrón noticed that the Devil appeared much bulkier than usual. A suspicious sign. Hmmmmmmmm. Unknown to the Devil, El Bizarrón changed his bed to a corner, a far corner. And waited.

At midnight he heard the clangor of falling rocks. At once he shouted, *"Ay,* what a mosquito has bitten me!"

Naturally the Devil thought, two boulders have dropped on him and to this fellow they are no more than an insect bite. He was impressed. Disturbed. Shaken to his red marrow.

He climbed down to note exactly El Bizarrón's condition. This one was now sitting under the barbecue, unbruised, unscratched, unmarked. And there lay the smashed rocks.

27

"Ah," said El Bizarrón in a voice of wonder, "I believed it was a mosquito and instead it was these stones. How came they here?"

Now the Devil's teeth clacked with fright. Speaking between clacks he declared, "Fellow, I shall give you a burro loaded with silver if you will leave here—if you leave for a destination far, far away. Preferably the moon. Or farther."

El Bizarrón accepted the offer. Why not? He brought up the burro. The Devil filled the saddlebags with money, till they bulged like sacks of potatoes.

"There you have it. Now go."

El Bizarrón went. After he had been gone a while, the Devil's wife said to him, "That ninny deceived you. He is not so strong as all that." She flung sneers against the Devil as if she were hurling stones at a stray dog.

Her scorn convinced her husband. So, saddling a horse, he set out to find El Bizarrón and take from him the donkey and the riches.

Looking back, El Bizarrón glimpsed the Devil approaching at a distance. Quickly he hid the donkey in a field of sugarcane. Then he lay on his back in the middle of the road with his legs in the air.

The Devil came up. In astonishment he asked, "And what ails *you?*"

"Ah, nothing. That stubbornness of a donkey refused

28

to walk. So I gave him a kick that sent him above the clouds. . . ."

The Devil, his teeth clattering again, wanted to know, "But why are you lying here kicking at the wind?"

"I don't want the donkey killed when he drops back to earth. This way I'll ease his fall with my feet."

At that the palsy of the Devil's teeth affected the rest of him. He might have been a flag lashed by a gale. Swiftly he spurred his horse and galloped home.

His wife asked, "Did you catch him?"

"Catch him! Should I want to? There he was. No sign of the burro—he had kicked it to Heaven. And if I had waited to recover the money he might have booted *me* to Heaven. And what place is that for the Devil? Glad am I to be free of him."

From Cuba
Feijōo, Samuel. *Cuentos Populares Cubanos*

ANIMAL TALES

Brer Rabbit's Trickery

One day a man set out carrying a tray of meat.
 Brer Rabbit and Brer Monkey glimpsed him . . .
then didn't they have a conference! Words, plans, discussion, you do this, no, I'll do that and *you* do this, no, no, that won't do at all, at all, and finally out tumbled a scheme.

Brer Monkey hid himself away, totally away. Brer Rabbit pranced out of the brush big as life, maybe a lot livelier, and started a conversation with the man. What man? The man with the tray of meat, of course. Along they sauntered, discoursing now about this, now about that.

All of a sudden Brer Rabbit moaned, "Un, un, un, un, un, un!"

The man asked, "Brer Rabbit, what makes you go on like that, un, un, un, un, un, un?"

"That meat smells poorly, man, poorly. The sun shines hotly, the meat smells poorly. That's why I say un, un, un, un, un, un."

"Well, but Brer Rabbit, what do you want? It is my custom, carrying my meat so. Too bad it should worry you. But what can I do?"

"What can you do? I'll tell you what can you do. Tie it to a bit of string and haul it behind you. So far behind you the smell will float backward 'stead of forward."

"All right, man, anything for company, man." And the man went and tied a length of cord to the meat and dragged it behind him as if he were leading a dog. And along they sauntered, discoursing now about this, now about that.

Meanwhile, let us not forget Brer Monkey, who hid himself away, totally away. Now he unhid himself—but not to the man. Oh, no. Crawling and creeping, he loosed the meat from the cord and put in its place a rock. All the while the man and Brer Rabbit were sauntering and discoursing.

At last Brer Rabbit rolled an eye way around till it could view behind. He glimpsed a rock bumping over the ground. No sign of any meat at all, at all. Brer

Monkey had done his job just fine.

That old rabbit clutched himself and exclaimed, "Man, I forgot something! My wife told me to come and meet her at the pond. And here I am, miles away. I could bang myself for forgetting and coming so far!"

"I'm sorry you can go no farther with me, man. That was a fine discourse we had."

"Indeed it was, man," said Brer Rabbit, shaking his hand in the friendliest way.

As the man began to haul in his string Brer Rabbit

took off like a stone from a slingshot. Went flying along till he reached Brer Monkey hiding with the meat. On the way Brer Rabbit argued with himself about sharing that meat with Brer Monkey—and lost the argument.

He came up to Brer Monkey puffing and blowing like a sassy wind. "Is my throat dry, man! Dry as peanuts. Dry as pepper. I got to have some water. There's water up there, and here I go. Stop here with the meat till I come back, man."

Away he hopped—but not to the water. Only to a big

tree where he hid and watched to see if Monkey touched the meat. Monkey did not. After an immense time Rabbit hustled back, puffing and blowing as though he'd been running fifty miles.

"Well, Brer Monkey, what a drink I had! Being we're such good friends I left a drop for you."

"Where is it, man? Now I have such a thirst my throat's forgot how to swallow. Show me where that water is."

Brer Rabbit pointed. "You see that road yonder? Go shock, shock, shock up that road till you see a nice cool water. But do not finish it up, Brer Monkey. Leave some there!"

When Monkey had gone far but not too far, far enough not to see but not too far to hear, Rabbit took up a branch and began to lash the tree trunk. All the time he bellowed in a most distressed voice, "Oh, I beg your pardon, sir, 'twasn't me that stole your meat, sir, it was that Brer Monkey, believe me, sir!"

Hearing the lashing and the bawling, Brer Monkey skipped into the nearest tree and sailed away into the woods. And never came back. So Brer Rabbit had a feast all by himself.

From Montserrat
Parsons, Mrs. Elsie C. *Folklore of the Antilles, French and English*

The Goat and the Tiger

A Goat decided to build himself a house. A Tiger decided to build himself a house. Two like decisions. And would you believe it, happening at the same time. But then, what would a story be without coincidence?

The Goat tripped into the forest. He chose a clearing, chopped down a number of trees to use as beams and then, panting with well-deserved fatigue, he left.

Later that day the Tiger, in quest of a clearing, stumbled on one. Better still, he also stumbled over a neat pile of beams. (We know whose—but *he* didn't.)

"Fortune favors me!" he cried. Gleefully, using the hewn timbers, Tiger erected the framework of a house.

Satisfied with his efforts, he went away.

The following morning Goat arrived back at the clearing. Seeing the house frame already up, he threw up his hooves and cried, "Fortune aids me!" Contentedly he thatched the roof, then went off for a nap.

In the afternoon who should appear but? . . . Right. Tiger himself. Not at all surprised at Fortune's help, he set to work to plaster the walls.

When the house was completed each builder, believing himself to be Fortune's favorite as well as sole master of the house, went to move in. Goat arrived, bag and baggage. At midday Tiger flung open the door. What was his astonishment to find an enormous goat already established.

Goat exclaimed, "Good day, Tiger! Welcome to my fine new house! Welcome! Welcome! What may I do for you?"

Tiger swelled with rage. Goat swelled with displeasure —he could see *something* was wrong. And Tiger hesitated no more than from here to there to let Goat know what that was.

Said Goat, "*I* cut the posts. Fortune lent a stout arm. *I* thatched the roof. Fortune helped a bit more. *I* brought in furniture and myself—and now you, *insolent,* claim the house is yours!"

Tiger explained himself. "I wish to construct a house. *Bon? Bon.* Fortune guides me. I put up the framework.

I go away. Again gracious Fortune presents herself. I plaster the walls. And now *you* aspire to be the dweller!"

Much wrangling and argument. More argument and wrangling. Much, much more. At midnight both wrangler and arguer were exhausted. Their rights being equal, they were forced to decide that they must share the house. Share and share alike.

But each evening Tiger, in order to distress and annoy his crony (I use the term loosely), returned from his hunting burdened with a plump goat. Throwing the carcass on the ground, he would command in a lordly manner, "Fellow dweller, skin this! Skin this for me at once!"

It is correct to say Goat was annoyed and distressed. Enough to give himself up to bitter reflections. It was clear that through Tiger's strategy the number of Goat's relatives would decrease rapidly. Like beans from a sack when a hole appears.

Indeed yes, and so it was. The pruning of the herds went on at such a rate that soon scarcely a kid remained. Something had to be done. And quickly or not at all. Hmmmmmmm. Goat pulled on his beard in deep thought.

One night while Tiger was sleeping soundly his companion slipped out of the house. His steps directed themselves toward the cave of an old, old tiger, the biggest in the region. The cave sat high on a cliff. And this cliff sloped so steeply it was a wonder the cave didn't slide completely off.

On reaching the cave Goat was greeted by loud snores. Better snores than snarls, thought Goat. He crept into the cave. With a push he started the old tiger rolling out of the cave, over the cliff, down, down, down. Then down, down, down scampered Goat. Down to where the dead tiger lay. With a mighty heave he loaded the tiger on his back and returned home, panting with each slow step.

Goat's thump on the door resounded like a giant drum. Tiger bounced from his bed, all aquiver.

Throwing the carcass of the old tiger on the ground with dramatic force (it took his last dab of strength to do so), Goat ordered, "Brother, here is a tiger. Skin it! Skin it!"

Tiger trembled. (He couldn't believe his eyes.) Goat trembled. (His legs were giving out.) Without another word both fell onto their beds and pretended to fall asleep.

Have I mentioned that the beard of Goat was so long that it served him as a coverlet? If not, consider it mentioned. Now Goat pulled and yanked at his cover, making sure that Tiger heard him. Then, as if he were dreaming, this killer of tigers murmured, "Oh, tigers, tigers, more tigers! There is yet another tiger!"

The frightened Tiger cried out and inquired about his comrade's worry.

Goat hastened to reassure him. "It's really nothing, you know. This beard is quite uncivil and utters insults during my sleep. I cannot seem to control it at all, at all. But do not trouble yourself, friend, it is nothing, *absolument.*"

The two returned to sleep. At least as much to sleep as one can with only one eye closed.

Again the beard spoke, "I am hungry for tigers, let us seek out the rest of the tigers!"

It was too much. Tiger, abandoning house, furniture and companion, fled into the night. And so Goat became king of the kids, and soon the land was repopulated with goats.

From Haiti
Bastien, Rémy. *Anthologie du Folklore Haitien*

Compae Rabbit's Ride

Once Brer Tiger fell in love with Sis Fox, who didn't so much fall in love with *him*. Compae Rabbit learned of it. And sat himself down and put his mind to brewing up some devilment—which wasn't difficult for Rabbit. After a time he sashayed up to Sis Fox and made a bet with her that he could ride Tiger horseback past her house.

"Done!" cried Sis Fox, thinking *this* time Rabbit's out-wagered himself. They shook hands on it.

Well, one day Sis Fox said to Brer Tiger, "Tiger, I feel like dancing. What are you going to do about that?"

"I shall give a dance then, Miss Fox."

"And will you ask Compae Rabbit to play his banjo for us? He is the very best player in the *barrio*."

"That I will do," said Tiger. And he thought, if Compae comes to play and if during the dance the lights go out and if it is pitch dark and if there are scareful noises, then Compae Rabbit just might run down my throat by mistake. Yum!

So Tiger went to see Compae Rabbit about playing his banjo for the dance. And Rabbit said yes, if he were not in pitiful health he would play. Tiger, who had tasty dreams of Rabbit bouncing down his jaws, said, "Then I'll pick you up Saturday."

Come Saturday, Compae Tiger went to find Rabbit. When Rabbit saw him draw near he wrapped up his head with leaves. Around them he wound a big red kerchief till he looked like a knapsack ready to take off for a picnic.

Tiger knocked at the door and called, "I've come to get you for the dance, Rabbit."

"*Ayyyyyyyyy*, Compae Tiger! I am dying and that's a fact! Aches in my tooth. Aches in my head. And besides, a fever is burning me up."

"I will carry you then on my back."

"Very well, Compae Tiger." Rabbit climbed up one side of Tiger and fell off the other. "Ah, Tiger, you see how weak I am? Perhaps if I put on your back an old blanket I have here, I could stay on. What do you think?"

"Place it on."

Rabbit adjusted the blanket, hopped onto it and, pufffff! landed on the ground.

"Ay de mí, it doesn't work at all. . . ."

"Then, Compae Rabbit, do whatever you have to do in order to hold on."

"Maybe a bridle to hang onto . . . and a pair of baskets, one on each side that I will not fall off. . . ."

"By all means, lay them on."

So Rabbit harnessed Tiger, setting a bit into his mouth, fastening a rein, and buckling on himself, unseen by Tiger, a fine pair of spurs. Clamping his banjo under his arm, he leaped on Tiger's back. Flicked with his whip.

"What are you doing, Compae Rabbit?"

"Brushing flies off your neck, Tiger."

Flick, Flick.

"Now what are you doing, Rabbit?"

"Brushing flies off your flank."

Rabbit put the spurs to Tiger.

"What are you doing, Compae Rabbit?"

"I want to go faster. My head throbs like a bell tolling in a belfry."

Pricking with his spurs and flicking with his whip, Rabbit had Tiger sprinting like a racehorse.

They dashed right by Sis Fox's house where many people stood waiting for the music to begin. *"Adiós!"* cried Compae Rabbit, saluting Sis Fox with the whip.

Quickly he hopped off Tiger and tied him to a fence post. Like a common everyday horse. Then Rabbit threw away his sore head and ran inside the house and commenced plunking the banjo. And everyone danced—back and forth and round about.

Wolf came by. Poor Tiger said to him, "Compae Wolf, for the sake of heaven will you undo me?"

So Wolf untied Tiger and unsaddled him and Tiger slunk into the dance. "Compae Rabbit, play us a waltz and play it well," he growled.

"With pleasure, Compae Tiger. But while I play I'm going to sit here by the window where it's breezy and cool."

So Rabbit plunked with all his might while the guests waltzed with all their might. And suddenly the lights went out. And just as suddenly Rabbit went out—the window.

Thus Rabbit won his bet. And Tiger was so humiliated he kept well away from Compae Rabbit and Sis Fox for a long time to come. And that was a blessing for them both.

From Puerto Rico
Ramírez de Arellano, Rafael. *Folklore Portorriqueño*

The Tortoise Who
Flew to Heaven

Once, at the time when St. Peter was first made gate-keeper of Paradise, he persuaded le Bon Dieu to give a grand dinner in Heaven. They invited all the *bêtes à z'ailes* (a fancy name for winged creatures). It was the first time such an occasion had taken place. At all events, to continue my story—on the branches, around the nests, in the brush, no one spoke of anything else.

"Have you been invited to the banquet?"

"Mais, naturellement, and why should I not be invited?"

The big birds found, somewhat to their chagrin, that

St. Peter had even invited the tiniest of birds and insects, the hummingbird, the *cici z'hebes,* the honey fly, the firefly, the large night moth. These creatures themselves were well content that St. Peter had not forgotten them.

Of course only the winged ones had been invited. For St. Peter understood that the other animals would find it difficult to make the journey to Heaven. (No elevators in those days.) For their part, the animals themselves understood. They were not envious.

No. I must make one exception. Compère Tortoise was envious. He would have given his very shell—his smooth, shining shell of which he was very proud—to mount to Heaven and the banquet. Tortoise hated to be left out of *anything.* But he was a clever beast; he hid his envy and his plan. Plan? Oh yes, he had a plan. The planniest of. . . . Well. Enough of that.

Tortoise began by pretending that he had been invited. Whenever he ran into a four-footed animal he would ask, "Eh! Compère! You are attending the great banquet of le Bon Dieu and St. Peter, are you not?"

And the other would reply, "And how do you think we would arrive there? You can well comprehend why we have not been invited."

Tortoise would say, "Hmm. Hmm. That is droll, that, for they have invited *me.*"

All would laugh: *quia, quia, quia.* They asked, "Where

are your wings for flying? *Bref!*" They mocked him.

Compère Tortoise said nothing. He was determined to get to Heaven. If not by this way, by that.

The day of the banquet arrived. After the "pipiri," the chant of the pipiri bird that opened the gate of day, all the winged beasts began to ready themselves. They arranged their feathers, brushed their wings, brightened their colors. The butterflies touched up their patterns. One fly polished another.

Compère Tortoise slouched about among the *invités*. He put on a woeful air (most unusual for him).

Pigeon saw him and asked, "What is the matter, Tortoise?"

Compère Tortoise sighed. "Ah, what to do, my dear Pigeon. I am sad. My misery is barely supportable. I am just recovered—well, very nearly recovered—from a malady. Now I must replenish my provisions. But how? With what?"

"You are ill, Compère? For that reason you say nothing bad of anyone these last few days?"

(You must know that Tortoise suffered the reputation of being an ill-disposed fellow who had always some malice to say of someone. Which meant that little of good could be said about *him*.)

Tortoise affected a plaintive voice to speak to Pigeon. "Why do you say that, Compère? I have never said a mean thing of anyone. You well know that I am a poor *stupide*." (True. But Tortoise did not believe it, not for a moment.) "After such unkind words I do not dare ask you for a favor. I can see you are in a harsh mood today. Today of all days." A sob escaped him.

Pigeon was a good creature. He was touched. He said to Tortoise, "Compère, what I just said was in fun. A pleasantry, no more. If I am able to do anything for you, ask. I will do my best. Unhappily, I am not rich."

"What I wish is not a great thing. I would like you to lend me a few tiny feathers. They would serve me. If I cleaned and brushed them I could sell them to the four-footed folk for pillows. Thus I could earn enough to sustain me. How kind you are, Pigeon!"

Pigeon had never seen Tortoise so sweet. He decided he must indeed be very sorrowful to speak so gently. So he said, "Take them, my dear Tortoise, pick up all the feathers you want. I do not need them. On the contrary, I am *très content* that they will be of use to you."

And Pigeon himself aided Tortoise in gathering them. He tied them with a blade of grass and fastened them to Tortoise's shell.

"*Au revoir,* Pigeon, and many thanks," called Tortoise and crawled away.

Pretty soon he ran into Guinea Fowl—well, not exactly *into* him, for Tortoise never traveled that fast. Anyway,

Guinea Fowl didn't even see Tortoise he was so busy peeping through a clump of *ziccac* at Peacock.

Tortoise pretended not to notice what Guinea Fowl was doing. "Good day, Guinea Fowl," he said in a bright but low voice. "You appear well today—even beautiful. Much handsomer than Peacock. Peacock is inclined to consider himself quite an aristocrat. Merely because of that fancy tail. What a dandy! There are other birds far more magnificent. Take you, for instance, Guinea Fowl. You are certainly more elegant than Peacock. . . ."

At that Guinea Fowl fluttered about in the giddiest way. "Oh, do you think so, Tortoise? Really, *I* don't think so, but if *you* do. . . . Handsomer than *Peacock?* Well, well, I must say. . . . Yes, well, well. . . ."

Between flattery and flutterings, Tortoise managed to request a few old feathers. "Just to put into a medallion, Guinea Fowl." He managed to get a good quantity.

Then he made his way around the *ziccac* until he reached Peacock. At that moment he began laughing, *"Quia, quia, quia."*

Peacock looked up haughtily. "What ails you, Tortoise?" he demanded.

"It is that Guinea Fowl, Peacock! He just informed me that no bird is as handsome as he—none at all. He stands at the other side of this *ziccac* and primps before a mirror. Never have I seen such a conceited fowl!"

Peacock replied, "Guinea Fowl is a real silly. Has he never taken note of my tail?"

"As to that, Compère, it is true, no one has a tail like yours. Let me see it . . . spread it out a little . . . ah, those plumes one can only call gorgeous! Here are some on the ground. . . . Why do you ever throw them away, Peacock?"

Peacock simpered. "Those! They are old, worn-out feathers—no longer pretty at all. What would I do with them? Each day I am obliged to rid myself of some. I have so many! They sometimes make me ache with their heaviness. I would be happier to have fewer. It is true they are beautiful, but so burdensome to drag around. But what to do, Tortoise, what to do?"

"Ah, Peacock, how can you speak so? If only I possessed two or three to arrange in my parlor, how they would enhance it. . . ."

"Help yourself, Tortoise. What a child you are to want such ragged things. . . ." And Peacock, feigning indifference, watched with one eye to see that Tortoise chose the brightest.

Tortoise raked himself a good heap and then went on to find more birds—and, with one story or another, more feathers. When he had accumulated a cushionful—more, a bolsterful—of plumes he hid himself and them in a thicket. Then he began to dress himself as a bird.

With glue from the breadfruit tree he fastened wing

feathers about his feet, tail feathers around his tail, back
feathers on his back, breast feathers against his breast,
neck feathers around his scrawny neck. So smothered
was he in feathers that at a glance Tortoise appeared a
true winged creature—one straight out of a fairy tale, for
he was all colors of the earth. But this did not bother
Tortoise. Looking in the mirror he was charmed; what
a fine gypsy of a bird stared back at him!

The sun was high overhead. Tortoise flapped his feet
and took off—up and away—along the road to Heaven.

On arriving in Paradise he peeped into the enormous
banquet hall. All the chairs were occupied. Not even a

piano stool stood empty. Undoubtedly the chairs were counted. If he were to ask for one, zup! out would go Tortoise. And *down* would go Tortoise.

So still in good humor he followed the path to the kitchen. Delicious aromas swirled and danced together. Fish, fowl and meats turned on the spits. Plump loaves of bread nearly burst from their crusts. Fruits and vegetables of all varieties crowded each other in their dishes. Wine sparkled in strange-shaped bottles. Pies, tarts, cakes and sweetmeats tried to outdo one another in their height, shape and juiciness.

Tortoise fell into a chair. He waved to the nearest servant. "Come, come, I am starving from my long journey. Bring me . . . bring me . . . some of everything! And of some things more than some . . . that cherry tart, several slices of that suckling pig . . ." His mouth watered and his eyes rolled in his head.

When Tortoise could hold not a bite more he began to speak. And as usual with Tortoise, when he spoke he spoke too much.

The servants had thought it somewhat bizarre that such a majestic winged one should wish to eat in the kitchen. But who were they to object? However, as soon as they saw he was a bit tipsy they asked, "Why is it you are not in the dining room with the others?"

Tortoise began to laugh, his mouth splitting up to his ears. He was more than a bit tipsy. Much more.

"Would you believe how foolish these winged beasts can be? Who then do you judge that I am? Surely you do not take me for one of *them?* Ah, that is too much. I am no bird, I am a four-footed animal. And I have more spirit than any of them, winged or legged." Tortoise gave a little cough of importance.

"I made a wager that I would come here—and behold, here I am. As to these feathers—there was no trouble about *that.* The birds have such respect for me that they dance when I snap my fingers. . . . So when I said, 'Birds, I must have feathers,' there was not a protest except from one or two of the bigger birds and I simply *looked* at them. Ah, how they quaked! Inside of two breaths all were plucking out feathers like mad. It doesn't do to joke with Tortoise, you know. . . ." He gave two little coughs of importance.

"Well, my friends, I have eaten well. I have drunk well. Your coffee is excellent. Now if you will give me a sip of cognac and two or three cigars I will be on my way home. The sun is already low."

All this time the servants were coming and going between the kitchen and dining room. They could not imagine how such grand and solemn birds as Eagle and Falcon could tremble before that peppercorn of a Tortoise.

But their ears stretched open like hibiscus blossoms

when they heard Pigeon conversing with his friends. *"Mes amis,* now that we have dined so heartily perhaps we can muse a bit over the woeful ones of the world, in particular, Compère Tortoise. I saw him this morning. I found him truly repentant for his sharp tongue. I do not believe le Bon Dieu would begrudge our taking back something to our poor comrade."

The other birds who had been so flattered by Tortoise that morning agreed. "Pigeon is right. Tortoise has a sharp tongue. But since he is trying to curb it we should try to help him."

Only Compère Eagle disagreed with them. "Huh, huh. For my part, charity is all very well—but not for Tortoise. A dull fellow, that. However, do as it pleases you."

One of the servants was just serving Eagle. He had remarked three large eagle plumes on Tortoise's back. *Dégoûtant!* Disgusting! That such a lofty fellow as Eagle would *look* at Tortoise—after finding him so dull—let alone shake and shiver before him, plus lending him some feathers. . . . What was life on earth coming to? Muttering to himself he tipped the bottle of wine—not into the glass, but *(quelle horreur!)* over Eagle's wing.

Eagle turned on the servant a cold eye (as only eagles can). "Numbskull, can you not pay attention?"

The servant was indignant (or foolish) enough not to feel fear. He replied, "Ah! Ah! Do not speak to me so,

55

do you hear? I may be a *domestique* but I do not tremble before Tortoise. No, not I! Tortoise would not dare force me, *me,* to give him feathers! Never!"

Eagle sat bewildered. He understood not at all. "Huh, huh, what says this simpleton? Do any of you comprehend, sirs, what this one is saying?"

The servant still babbled away. "What I say is not too clever to be understood. I say that you do not mind scolding me, but this very morning you groveled before Tortoise, you, Compère Eagle, and these other big birds with you. Tortoise himself informed me—and the other servants heard him as well. And if you peck me I shall defend myself!"

The silly had just finished speaking when the door opened. Who should appear but Tortoise. So full of his own consequence was he that instead of taking the outside door to leave on his journey he had by mistake opened the door to the dining room. And there he stood in the middle of his feathers, eyed by all.

At first the birds did not recognize him.

But then, *"Good* evening, Compère Eagle! Good evening, Peacock. Good day, Pigeon, Cici. . . . How is everyone? Will no one give me a good evening?" Tortoise bowed and strutted about like a clown. A wellfeathered clown.

They sat in a state of shock until Eagle rose and advanced toward Tortoise. "Tell me, Tortoise, huh, huh, is this *your* affair? The servant informs me that you boast in the kitchen of making all of us quiver before you. True, Tortoise?"

"Not true," gasped Tortoise, turning from pompous to pallid. And he spun about to rush from the room. Only to find the servants had closed the door.

Tortoise saw that he was cornered. He cried again, "The story is untrue. As untrue as . . . as four-footed creatures can fly!"

"Huh, huh, and you say *that* is untrue, Tortoise?"

The servants cried in their turn, "Our account is true! It is you who speak untruly."

Never had there been such an uproar in le Bon Dieu's dining room. Fortunately, le Bon Dieu had shortly before excused Himself, and St. Peter was checking the gates for the evening.

At the end, the servants were so convincing that the *bêtes à z'ailes* all realized that Tortoise had invented a tremendous myth. *And* had deceived them. Ah, what rage!

They jumped on Tortoise. Such blows from beaks, such tears from talons! They yanked off his feathers, they batted his shell. They ended by dropping him on the floor, half-dead. A *domestique* snatched him up and gave him a good kick which sent him tumbling into the corridor.

When Tortoise recovered his senses (he had lost them

during the battle) he found himself bruised and beaten, the feathers lying here and there. He wept.

Then he felt a light touch on his foot. There crouched Zagrignain, the spider. She spoke to him.

"Ah, Tortoise, will you never learn? You must stop looking for ways to raise yourself from the earth. But now you must leave quickly before the birds find you here. They are still angry enough to make a soup of you. . . . Come along."

In spite of his soreness Tortoise managed to drag himself to the back door. He stuck his head out. And then he drew it back, shivering.

Zagrignain cried, "Well, well, why do you wait? This flock will return—and then! Go, Tortoise, go!"

Tortoise had not the strength to speak. His mouth opened and shut, shut and opened, but released no words. He beckoned Zagrignain to come. She peered out.

Before the door was a vast blue hole. The bluest of blue. And far, far away, at the end of it they saw a little green ball. It was the earth.

"Ah, I see! They have pulled off your wings, and you can no longer fly. Yes, yes, that is a problem. Then I must help you escape, in some way. And there is only one way I know of. I will hold you with my eight legs, attach my thread to the floor of Paradise and we will both drop to earth. But you must take care to remain quiet. A spider's thread is not a cable; it can break."

Tortoise dared not say yes. And yet he dared not say no. Finally he nodded a yes, which took less effort than shaking a no.

Zagrignain made Tortoise turn over on his back. She tied his four feet together strongly. Next, she fastened her thread to the keyhole of the back door. And then she sat herself down on Tortoise's feet.

"Attention, Tortoise! Let yourself fall sweetly into the abyss."

But Tortoise did not budge; he was frozen with fright.

Zagrignain pushed just enough to slide them over the floor of Heaven into the blue hole. Together they fell like a stone.

"Softly," called the spider. "Now that the wind has caught us we will ride more slowly."

It was true, they were not plummeting so fast. Fathom by fathom Zagrignain let out the thread. They descended.

Still Tortoise was not tranquil. "Such a delicate thread. . . . it will never hold us . . . you perhaps, but not me."

All the while Zagrignain paid out the thread.

After a bit, Tortoise took courage. He opened one eye. He saw Zagrignain releasing thread, more thread. . . . He asked suddenly, "Tell me, Compère, where do you find all this thread?"

"Silence, *ami,* I am very busy. . . ."

But the matter of the thread intrigued Tortoise. *"C'est drôle!* It is droll that one so small can hide away such lengths of thread. . . ." Then he began to laugh. It seemed Tortoise had recovered.

He began to sing, *"Butterfly is a creature of wings."* More softly, *"Zagrignain is a creature of thread."* More loudly, *"Hummingbird is a creature of feathers."* And softly again, *"Spider is but a creature of thread."*

Zagrignain was a trifle deaf. "What are you singing?"

Tortoise replied, "The Song of Butterfly. Do you not know it?"

He sang again,

"*Butterfly, a creature of wings,*
Spider, a mere spool of thread,
Hummingbird, a creature of feathers,
Spider, only a spool, a spool, a spool."

Tortoise was so content with his rude song that he sang louder and louder.

At last the little spider heard. Her spinning ceased. They swung in the air. And as he came eye to eye with Zagrignain, Tortoise stopped his chanting.

He knew she had understood his impudent song. In terror he cried, "No, no, Zagrignain, I did not mean it, it is not true . . ."

Zagrignain regarded Tortoise in disgust. And then she let go of him.

Tortoise fell down, down, down, down until he landed bo! on a rock. His shell shattered.

Despite his tumble Tortoise was not dead. But from that time on his smooth shell, of which he had been so proud, was marked with thirteen sections. A just punishment, and one with some effect. For we never again hear of Tortoise trying to fly—or planning to fly—or even *wishing* to fly. On the contrary, he always hugs the ground closely.

From the Antilles
Georgel, Thérèse. *Contes et Légendes des Antilles*

Rabbit's Long Ears

At the beginning of Creation—or rather, at the *end* of Creation—Rabbit, with ears as small as *frijoles,* came to stand before the Creator. He had a grievance. Such a grievance.

"Creator, sir," he began.

"Yes, Rabbit?" spoke the Creator.

"Ah, so you can really see me then. It doesn't always háppen. Indeed no. As a matter of fact, it doesn't *often* happen."

"*What* doesn't often happen?" asked the Creator, mystified.

"That anyone can see me. It's my size. You were ungenerous with that when you came to me. Most ungenerous. About other things I have no complaint. Lavish you were with speed. . . . So with softness. . . . Most of all with handsomeness." (Rabbit was inclined to be vain.)

"*But*—what are speed, softness and handsomeness if they cannot be seen? It's not that I am greedy about size. It would be nice, of course, to be as big as Elephant or Camel. Fancy what a picture I'd make with my size, my speed, my softness, my suppleness, my style, my symmetry. . . ."

The Creator coughed.

"What I mean is," continued Rabbit hurriedly, "if I were Goat's size, no more, I should be content. Quite, quite content." A tear dribbled off his nose.

The Creator thought. He had been so busy creating He hadn't had much time for thinking lately. (It's no easy matter creating a world.) So now, chin in hands, He pondered the problem. A ticklish question. Each animal had been measured out a certain amount of size. A goodly amount to Elephant. A poorly amount to Ant.

If, for example, He were to take away a fraction of Whale's size to give to Rabbit, Whale would be unhappy; he liked being the biggest creature in the world. If He borrowed from Camel to give to Rabbit, Camel might sulk. Sulky by nature, he almost certainly would sulk. Might even refuse to be a beast of burden. He might borrow a pinch from Grasshopper—but that would mean no more Grasshopper. The Creator sighed. (It's no easy matter creating a world—and creatures. Especially discontented creatures.) Then an idea drifted into His mind.

"Rabbit," He said briskly, "it has just occurred to me that if you really and truly want to be bigger, you will be willing to work for it. So here is your chore: bring me the feather of an eagle, the tooth of a lion, the egg of a serpent. Then we shall see. I just may present you with an extra dose of size. Though I won't promise."

Now it was Rabbit's turn to ponder. Not for long. Rabbit had speedy thoughts as well as speedy legs. First he picked a gourd. Then he made a whistle of the gourd. After that he went whistling over the mountain, sounding like North Wind himself.

Before too long Eagle glided down beside Rabbit. "What's this? What's this noise?" he demanded.

"Do not excite yourself, Eagle. It's a hair from my hide that insists on whistling once a day. When it does, a troop of animals appears, that I may choose one of them for my dinner. Unfortunately, animals are not to my liking. A pity. Perhaps in a million years or so I may acquire a taste for animals. Meanwhile, they chase me. Oh, Eagle, give me one of your feathers. Then they will respect me. In return, where you pluck out the feather, there I will sow my whistling hair. May it do *you* some good."

Eagle agreed to the exchange gladly. After all, *he* didn't have to wait a million years to acquire a taste for animals. Although he did not know it, it might take that long to acquire his next meal—in case he depended on the whistling hair.

So feather was traded for hair. With the feather stuck behind his ear, Rabbit thumped over the mountain as drumsticks thump on a drum. *"Pito, pito,"* he whistled.

Out of the thorny scrub crawled Serpent. "What is this-s-s-s?" she hissed.

Rabbit recounted the same tale he had told Eagle. "A hair from my side . . . a flock of animals, appetizing little animals such as mice, rats, monkeys . . . when what I crave is a tasty egg. . . ."

Serpent's mouth watered. Inside of a moment and a half she was grasping the whistling hair and inviting Rabbit to help himself from the nest. Away frisked Rabbit with the egg tucked in one ear and the feather poked jauntily behind the other.

Lion, dozing before his cave, heard the *pito, pito,* of a gourd whistle. "From where comes this far-from-mellifluous sound?" he roared, making a ferocious face at Rabbit.

Rabbit was undaunted by faces, ferocious or other-

wise. "It is a hair from my side that whistles up my dinner, or what would be my dinner if I dined on *animalitos* instead of succulent sprouts, roots and herbs. These creatures would soon respect me if I showed them a tooth of yours, Lion. A tooth you wouldn't need, Lion, if I give you my whistling hair. It will guide your meal directly into your gullet, Lion."

Lion was charmed with the idea of food leaping into his jaws with no effort on his part. The tooth was yanked out and handed over to Rabbit. The magic hair was quickly twined into his own fur. Lion went off to await the first course. As waits go, it was not a short one.

Meanwhile, Rabbit arrived with his luggage before the Creator, whose eyes bulged. *"Ay,* Rabbit! When you with your size can accomplish such deeds, what would you manage with the size of Camel or Goat? With reason, the rest of the creatures would plague me for protection—or for more size. No, Rabbit, what is not needed in the world is a large-sized, or even a medium-sized, rabbit. As you are, you are formidable enough."

Rabbit looked so disappointed that the Creator gave a great sigh. Reaching out, He took hold of Rabbit's ears. Pulled. And pulled. Pulled some more. Until the ears had stretched out the length of an ear of corn.

"Vaya, Rabbit. Now you possess speed, softness, handsomeness—and sizable ears. As for more bigness for you—it would only make a trouble in the world. And enough of those we have already."

So Rabbit rambled off, satisfied at least that his ears were an impressive size even if the rest of him was not.

From Cuba
Guirao Ramón. *Cuentos y Leyendas Negras de Cuba*

ANNANCY TALES

Brother Annancy
Fools Brother Fire

One day Brother Dry Grass and Brother Fire had a dispute. About what? Oh, maybe about which one was more important in the village—or who wore prettier clothes—or which was less wet than the other—*I* don't know.

Anyway, Fire was so fired up after the argument he stopped at the café to see his friend Annancy. He felt he had to let off some steam (though in this case it was smoke). He might have been smarter to let it off somewhere else, for Annancy was a better friend to Dry Grass than to *him*.

68

After crackling and fuming for some time, Fire said, "Brother Annancy, tomorrow I'm going to burn that fellow Dry Grass up."

Annancy thought for a while. Then he said, "Brother Fire, when you are ready to go, call for me at the market. I shall fashion myself a whistle of bamboo. When we near the place of Dry Grass I will blow that whistle. In this way we will let him know we are coming."

So Fire went home for the night. And Annancy busied himself. He made the whistle. He also made a bargain with Brother Water; any time he heard that whistle blow he was to come down like rain.

The next morning Fire collected Annancy and away they went. Close to Dry Grass's home Annancy puffed on his shell.

Fire stopped. "Look there, Brother Annancy! Rain coming!" He sounded peevish. "Better I head for home. This is no day for getting even—or wet." So he left Annancy.

But on the way back Rain pattered along beside Fire. "So, Brother Fire, you aim to fight Dry Grass? Annancy told me to come and help so we could manage you. And we did, hey, Brother Fire?"

Fire, who had a hot temper, got angry. "So! That Annancy is interfering with my business? I'll stop and see him this minute. Point me out his yard."

So Water did that, and Fire entered Annancy's yard. "Brother Annancy, take heed. I'm going to pay you a little call next week."

"By all means, Brother Fire. With pleasure. I shall expect you."

"And, Brother," continued Fire, "so I don't lose the way, hang a line of clothes in your yard. Then I'll know it's your house."

"That I will do, Brother Fire. Depend on it."

And Fire went on his way.

Annancy laughed, but his wife was frightened. "Husband, you must do something to stop Fire from coming."

"Ah, no, wife, Fire is my good friend, my best friend. He can come and go as he pleases."

Next week Annancy went to visit Tiger, who lived close by. At his door he found a basket of laundry, freshly soaped and rinsed.

"Brother Tiger, see how damp these clothes are? You want them to mold? Better you hang them in the sun as quickly as possible."

Tiger went and hung the laundry on a line across the yard. And there it rippled and fluttered like a row of white ducks on a choppy pond.

Along came Fire roaring like a lion, and with him his friend Breeze. "See, Brother," hissed Fire, darting toward the clothes, "here is that fellow Annancy's yard."

Then Breeze blew like a hurricane and hurried as fast as one. And Fire leaped and skipped and drew nearer and nearer.

Tiger ran out into his yard and cried, "Turn back, you red-faced rascal! I can do without your company!"

But Fire was racing now at full speed.

Tiger bawled for Fire to stop. Fire paid no attention. He reached the yard and burned up Tiger's clothes and house. Then he turned back home, well satisfied.

And Annancy just laughed and sang,

"Fire and Breeze, they pay a call, oh!
A fine call they pay, ho, ho!
A call on the wrong house, oh,
Not Annancy's house, ho, ho!"

From Jamaica
Jekyll, Walter, ed. *Jamaican Song and Story*

Man-Crow

Once the whole world was in darkness. Why? Because of a big black bird named Man-Crow, who lived in the woods.

The King got tired of living in darkness (who could see his crown with everything so black?). So he offered thousands of pounds to anyone who would kill the bird and bring back the light. Then he thought again of all that darkness . . . and he offered one of his three daughters along with the thousands of pounds. Then he reached out and *felt* that darkness . . . and he promised that if someone would kill the bird, he would give that someone thousands of pounds, a daughter to marry and, make him a very rich man for the rest of his life.

At that, thousands of soldiers marched into the woods

to kill Man-Crow. They searched and they searched. And finally they found him on one of the tallest trees in the woods—way up high, almost out of sight. So nobody could kill him, and all the soldiers came back home. And settled down again in the darkness.

Only one person did not settle down and that was a little cocky fellow called Soliday. Soliday said to his grandmother, "Grandmother, I am so poor I am going to the woods to try and kill Man-Crow."

His grandmother scoffed. "Tche, boy, better you take a nap by the fire than go off to the woods and turn dead."

But Soliday paid her no heed. "Grandmother, I am off to town to buy me a bow and six arrows." And he went to Kingston and bought them.

Back at home he asked his grandmother, "Grandmother, roast me six johnnycakes if you will." And he put them in a knapsack and struck out for the woods.

In the woods he searched and searched until he came to a tall, tall tree and there in the tallest part of it perched Man-Crow.

Then Soliday called to him with this song:

> *"Good marnin' to you, Man-Crow,*
> *Good marnin' to you, Man-Crow,*
> *Good marnin' to you, Man-Crow,*
> *How are you this marnin'?"*

And the bird answered him,

74

"Good marnin' to you, Soliday,
Good marnin' to you, Soliday,
Good marnin' to you, Soliday,
How are you this marnin'?"

Then Soliday shot one of his arrows at Man-Crow so that it nicked him and two of his feathers came out. And Man-Crow hopped down to a lower bough.

Soliday sang again,

"Good marnin' to you, Man-Crow,
Good marnin' to you, Man-Crow,
Good marnin' to you, Man-Crow,
How are you this marnin'?"

And Man-Crow sang back as before,

"Good marnin' to you, Soliday,
Good marnin' to you, Soliday,
Good marnin' to you, Soliday,
How are you this marnin'?"

Once more Soliday loosed an arrow and once more two feathers flew out and once more Man-Crow jumped down to a lower branch. And this singing and shooting went on for some time with the same things happening: arrow, feathers, hop, song. Until five arrows were gone.

Now all this time Brother Annancy, that rackle-headed fellow, sat in another tree and watched what was going on.

By the time Soliday aimed his sixth arrow Man-Crow was halfway down that tree. And *this* time Soliday shot

Man-Crow so he dropped all the way down from that tree. Dropped down dead as dead.

Soliday ran straight up to him and cut out his golden tongue and golden teeth and shoved them in his pocket and ran right home to tell his grandmother.

And while he was doing that, Annancy climbed down from his tree as quick as quick. He threw that big bird Man-Crow over his shoulder and started off through the bush. He tramped and he tramped and he tramped until he arrived all scratched and breathless at the King's gate. *Kok, kok, kok,* he rapped.

"Who's there?" they asked.

"Me, Mr. Annancy," he said.

"Come in," they said.

In a while Annancy stood before the King. "What do you want?" asked the King.

"I am the one who killed Man-Crow."

Well! You should have seen the goings-on. Gold coins for Annancy, fine clothes for Annancy, the best bed in the palace for Annancy (except for the King's, of course), the most food Annancy had ever seen—*and* a princess for a wife and a big table in the dining room for him and all his relatives.

Only Annancy wouldn't sit at his table. He sat in the doorway to watch for Soliday (though he hoped with all his heart he wouldn't come). By then the King felt sure Annancy was up to some trick, but he didn't know what.

Directly Annancy saw Soliday approaching he excused

himself. And quick as quick he went into the kitchen.

Soliday knocked at the gate.

"What do you want?" they asked.

"I am the boy who killed Man-Crow."

"Go along, boy. Impossible! Mr. Annancy killed Man-Crow."

"I must see the King. Right away."

So they let him in. Soliday took from his pocket the golden teeth and tongue and showed them to the King.

"How can a bird live without a tongue or teeth?"

Everybody looked in the bird's mouth and sure enough, gone were teeth and tongue.

They called Annancy. "Annancy! Annancy! Come out, you Annancy!"

He called back, "I will soon be there."

As he wasn't soon there, they called again.

"I don't feel so well." And Annancy shut the kitchen door. He was so ashamed that quick as quick he worked to make a hole in the shingle to get away.

They called again, "You, Annancy! Come out of there!" And they pushed open the kitchen door.

By then Annancy was hidden in the shingle and there he is to this day. The King married Soliday to another daughter and made him one of the richest men in the world.

From Jamaica
Jekyll, Walter, ed. *Jamaican Song and Story*

Snake the Postman

One day Annancy asked Snake to be his postman. "For free? For free, Brother Annancy? Oh, no, I can't do that. I got to live, you know. But I might consider it for a salary, Brother Annancy, I just might."

"Hmmmm, Brother Snake, hmmmm. Seeing that you are one who loves blood, Brother, I will give you a bite off my head, Brother, each time you bring me my mail."

Snake agreed to that. Yes, indeed, very quickly he agreed to that.

The first night he delivered Annancy's mail he gave him a good bite in the head. Good for Snake. Not so good for Annancy, who suffered a bad pain in the head for the rest of the night. Being unable to sleep he gave the matter much cogitation. Not to mention reflection.

So the second night at mail delivery time Annancy invited his old friend Mr. Rabbit to come for a visit. A fine *long* visit. To express his welcome, Annancy gave up his snooze place to Mr. Rabbit . . . did it with no fuss, no regrets at all. Moved from the breezy hall to a little old dark corner. A corner so dark nobody could see into it.

"Now, Brother Rabbit," said Annancy briskly, "you will have your bed out in the hall, the nice cool hall. Just one thing, Brother Rabbit. A cousin of mine is sleeping here, too, and will come in later on. When you hear him call just get up and open the door to make sure who it is. That's not much to ask, hey, Brother Rabbit?"

And away he went and carried off the lamp.

But Rabbit thought, though he didn't say so, that it might not be *much* to ask but it was a *curious* thing to ask. The more he meditated on it the more suspicious he grew. This Annancy is up to some trick, he told himself. (Rabbit being an old trickster himself.) And he mused and suspected and mused some more till he happened at last on a decision.

He commenced digging a hole in the hall and he dug and dug and dug. After a time that hole fit Rabbit like his own skin. So he wore that hole down, down, down; and then up, up, up, until he found himself outside the hall and inside his own backyard.

Along came Snake in the darkness carrying a letter and shooting his tongue in and out, out and in, in anticipation of the juicy bite off Annancy's head.

"Brother Annancy!" he called outside the door.

Annancy heard him—but he didn't give answer. And Snake, growing hungrier, cried louder and louder.

Finally Annancy had no choice but to call back, "Coming, Brother Snake!" But coming was the last thing he intended to do.

What a sound sleeper that Rabbit is, he thought. "Cousin Rabbit," he called softly. Humph! Nobody could hear that.

"Godfather Rabbit," he called louder, so sweetly you could have licked it. Still no answer. Was Rabbit vexed at being awakened?

"Brother Rabbit!" shouted Annancy. That fellow wouldn't know if a hurricane hit him.

"Poppa! Poppa Rabbit!" bellowed Annancy.

How could Rabbit hear, being snug in his burrow a mile away? Of course, Annancy didn't know that—yet.

Crawling out of his safe, dark corner Annancy lighted his lamp and crept into the hall to search for Rabbit. There was a pile of dirt sitting there but no Rabbit. Oh, was Annancy sorrowful!

He wept, cried and complained to Snake that that first bite of his had mashed up the whole of his head. After

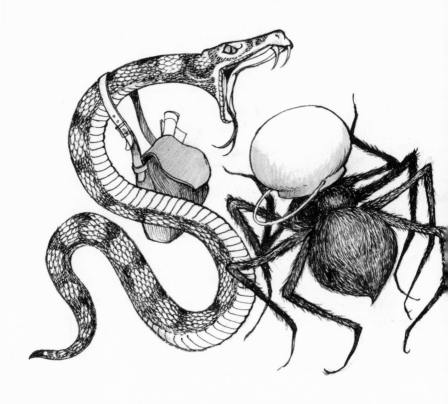

the next bite he wouldn't have a bit of head left. All this time Snake waited patiently at the door.

Annancy, walking up and down the hall, set himself to studying a scheme. Then he caught up a black pot and turned it down over his head.

As he put his head out the door, Snake, so hungry he couldn't see straight, bit the pot, thinking it was Annancy's head. Uhhhhhhh! Talk about jarring somebody's teeth! Snake's whole mouth was jarred. Sore, too. And his head was ringing. When he got home he sent word to Annancy he was sick and couldn't manage to come back another night.

Annancy himself was glad as a gull and sent back a message that he also was in bed. And from that day Snake broke friendship with Annancy.

From Jamaica
Jekyll, Walter, ed. *Jamaican Song and Story*

Wheeler

One day Puss started out on a journey and traveled till he came to a river. Being afraid of water, he couldn't cross the river. So he climbed a tree and went to sleep in it. And there he was, with a ringside seat for what happened next.

Well, what did happen next? That's just what I'm going to tell you, and it has to do with Annancy.

Annancy went fishing. Right under the tree where Puss was lying, but Puss didn't tell Annancy that. Didn't let on he was anywhere around.

Annancy didn't meet up with any fish. However, he did meet up with a licking stump, with honey oozing out and trickling down the trunk. Annancy licked and licked till that stump was polished pretty clean. Instead of leaving well enough alone, Annancy shoved his hand inside the trunk to squeeze out more honey. Instead of that, something squeezed *him*. And held on for dear life.

Annancy pulled and yanked and tugged. Not one pull, not one yank, not one tug got him anywhere at all. So in a quivery voice he asked, "Who got hold of me?"

A voice in the stump said, "Me, Wheeler."

"Awwwwwwww . . . let me see you wheel me then."

Whoever it was flung him, spun him and wrung him over a mile distant. Annancy landed—alive but not too happy. Not too unhappy either, the more he thought about it. He shook his head and said aloud but not *to* anybody, "I met with a little accident, no doubt about it, but I consider that little accident going to make a living for me and my family."

And home traipsed Annancy and found him some lovely iron pegs, not so pretty to look at, but *hard*. He carried them back to the riverbank where he had fallen after his flight and planted them right there in that very spot.

Nobody saw him but Puss, and Puss was so quiet he might have been Nobody.

Annancy left that place and crept back close to Wheeler and his stump. There he stayed, silent as Puss, until along

85

came Peafowl. Then Annancy called out, cheerful-like, "Brother Peafowl, guess what? A living is here for me and you."

"What's that, Mr. Annancy, what's that?"

Annancy guided Peafowl over to the hole in the tree. "See that hole, Brother Peafowl? As your hand is so long, just shove it in there now, don't be afraid, and you will find something grand."

Without pausing a second, Peafowl rammed his hand into the hole. Wheeler grabbed him.

"What's this, Mr. Annancy, what's this?"

"Just pull, Brother Peafowl, just pull. Hard now."

Peafowl pulled all right but he couldn't get away. And that Annancy was so proud of himself he chuckled inside him like a fresh little spring.

"Now, Brother Peafowl, you say, 'Who holds me here?'"

Peafowl did.

And the answer was the same as before. "Me, Wheeler."

"Now, Brother," instructed Annancy, "you say, 'Wheel me a mile and distant.'"

Peafowl did.

Wheeler flung him, spun him and wrung him a mile distant, and Peafowl landed directly on the iron pegs. Too bad for Peafowl. Good for Annancy, though. He ran up and stuck Peafowl in his bag.

Then he went back to his old place under a bush and

sat quiet. No one saw him at all, at all except Puss, and *he* didn't say a word.

Pretty soon who should come along but Rat.

"Am I glad to see *you,* Brother Rat," said Annancy.

"What for?" asked Rat.

"Nothing to be afraid of, Brother Rat. A living is here for you and me. Come take a look."

Annancy carried Rat off to show him the stump.

"This is the living?" asked Rat.

"This is it, man. Shove your hand in the hole and you will find a living."

Rat stuck his hand in the hole, and Wheeler held him.

"Pull, Brother, pull!" cried Annancy.

"Doesn't do any good," said Rat.

"Then say, 'Who holds me?'"

Rat did.

"Me, Wheeler."

"Now say, 'Wheel me a mile distant.'"

So Rat did what he shouldn't have done—and landed against the iron pegs in no time at all. Annancy went and picked him up and put him in his bag along with Peafowl and went back to his hiding place.

After a while Puss came down from his tree and walked through the bush to the river. When he had gone down it aways he turned back and walked toward Annancy, coming up very meek and poorly.

Annancy felt gladness all through him when he saw

Brother Puss approach. "Walk up, my bold friend Mr. Puss. Come and see the living that is here for me and you."

Puss pretended he didn't know anything about it.

"Here now, Brother, see this stump? Just shove your hand into the hole and you'll find us a living."

But Puss played like he couldn't see the hole.

Annancy, very vexed, cried, "Shove your hand in so, man! Shove it in so! There, there, right where I'm pointing!"

Puss just thrust his hand in another direction as if he couldn't see the hole at all. And he went on and on, pretending to be too stupid to see the hole or understand Annancy.

Finally Annancy made such a flourish with his hand that it slipped in the hole . . . and Wheeler caught it. Annancy began to cry; he knew the danger down below.

"Run down to the river for me, good Brother Puss. There you will find some iron pegs, which you are to pull up for me."

Puss began to walk in his slinkly, sneaky way in the direction of the river, but he didn't go far. Just out of Annancy's sight. Then he took a good rest under a bush. After a bit he yawned and crept back to Annancy.

"All pulled up," he announced.

Annancy wouldn't believe him and, still crying, bade him return and fetch back one of his pegs for him to see.

Puss set out, took another snooze behind a tree and came back to Annancy. No iron peg.

"Where is that peg, Brother Puss?"

"Too heavy to carry, Brother Annancy, but I rolled it well out of the way."

"You fooling me, Brother Puss? You rolled those pegs far, far out of the way? Truly, Godfather Puss?"

At last Puss convinced him. Or maybe Annancy convinced himself. "Who holds me?" he asked.

"Me, Wheeler."

"Go on then, wheel me a mile distant."

Annancy flew through the air and dropped slam on his own trap. And Puss walked down and picked up Annancy and rammed him in the bag with Peafowl and Rat and carried off all the living.

From Jamaica
Jekyll, Walter, ed. *Jamaican Song and Story*

A TI MALICE TALE

Malice, Bouki and Momplaisir

Once there was a King who owned a kid by the name of Momplaisir. This Momplaisir was the favored animal of the herd. The softest clover for his bed. A silver bell fastened about his neck. Delicacies from the fingers of the King himself. And plump . . . ah! As a gourd.

One fine day Malice, the master tailor and a rogue to boot, stole Momplaisir and killed him. From his flesh he prepared a rich stew. He tanned the hide.

The grief of the King was terrible. He dispatched his guards to seek out the culprit. In vain. The guards pleaded, they threatened, without success. No one could point out the criminal for the good reason that no one knew who he was. Beside himself with sorrow, the King offered a fortune to anyone giving the merest hint as to how to identify the assassin.

As Malice was, naturally, the one able to reveal the fate of Momplaisir, and as he was a greedy rascal with a longing for riches, he decided on a course of action. From Momplaisir's hide he fashioned a superb jacket. Then he visited his friend Nock Bouki, who was as simple as one plus two.

Malice said to him, "Nock, I have a piece of news for you. It seems that the King is interviewing anyone familiar with the whereabouts, the whenabouts, the howabouts of his pet kid Momplaisir. I am off now to the court to hear the gossip. I'll keep you informed."

At the gate of the palace a crowd was gathered. Malice took his place at the end of the line and waited. When his turn came he said, "King, I have information. *Real* information. May I speak with safety of your beloved kid?"

The King answered, "On my word of honor, my good fellow, nothing unpleasant will befall you. Speak with all confidence."

Malice, feigning timidity, spoke, "King, to put you on the track of Momplaisir, it will be necessary to offer a great banquet, with fine food, drink and music. Allow each guest the opportunity to express by word and tune his grief caused by the loss of Momplaisir. Thus, I swear to you, you will trap the guilty one."

After some reflection the King agreed to the idea, saying, "If the plan succeeds, you will receive the royal reward. If the plan fails, Malice, you will suffer the royal displeasure; I am not wealthy. The expenses of such a feast will empty my treasury."

Malice accepted the risk and bowed his way out of the royal presence.

Then he went to visit Bouki, carrying his splendid jacket. "My dear Nock," he said, "the King is preparing a feast where enough food will be served to suffice one of us five years. The fashionable guests, those most elegantly dressed, will, of course, have the choice of the finest tidbits. Moreover, he who sings to the taste of the King will receive five barrels of silver. Look you, my dear Nock, I have already designed my costume and composed my song," and he displayed his jacket to the eyes of the envious Bouki.

With a sigh he continued, "I deplore my small appetite, for such a jacket would win me the entire meal plus the chief cook himself."

Bouki, his mouth watering, moaned, wailed and whined. "And what good will all this goodness do *me?* All will be well dressed except me. All will stuff themselves except me. At most I shall receive a chunk of tough mutton or pork—nothing dainty. *Non!* Better that I absent myself from such a fancy affair." He wiped a tear from his eye.

From under lowered lids he darted quick glances at Malice. After a moment's thought he proposed slyly, "My dear Malice, why not sell me this jacket of yours? On you it appears just a trifle loose. . . ."

"Nock, I would consent gladly only, as you know, my trade brings in few *centimes* so that I am poor, oh so poor. However, as a close friend, I might let you have it for the price of one barrel of silver."

"I will buy it," Bouki replied promptly.

"Next, I must advise you, Nock, to compose a song."

"Ah, why fatigue myself? Sell me yours."

"With pleasure, for another cask of silver."

"Done!" cried Bouki, thinking happily of the royal prize.

Armed with patience, Malice succeeded in three days in teaching Bouki the song along with the appropriate gestures. All was ready. It was necessary only to await the banquet.

The day before the celebration Malice put Bouki through a last rehearsal. Then he secretly visited the King.

"King," he said, "open your ear to the songs of your guests, for it is in this way that you will learn the sad fate of Momplaisir. But once the culprit is discovered, take care that he speaks no further. The scoundrel is a sorcerer capable of disappearing when he recites a simple formula. Your men must gag him the moment he reveals himself."

The King took careful note of this counsel.

The following evening there arrived at the court of the King an immense mob, all dressed in their best, all murmuring verses and all hungry as vultures. In the huge fireplaces whole carcasses of steers, calves, hogs and sheep turned on the spits. Row upon row of barrels spouted wine, *tafia* and fine rum. *Quelle magnificence!*

Bouki marched in, conceited as a *duc* in his finery. Like a peacock he fluffed up his jacket and turned himself for the inspection of the King. Then he sat himself down, in the front row.

The singing competition commenced. The guests took their turns. At each couplet a few of the King's men danced around the singer. Why, everyone wondered. Ah, they would see.

Malice slipped behind Bouki and whispered to him, "Make ready, my dear Nock, it is time to end the match, the food is giving out."

Bouki leaped to his feet and, holding out the fringes of his jacket (Malice had taught him the proper technique), he sang,

> *"King, I have learned that you give a feast,*
> *But you did not invite me, Nock Nack,*
> *And I hear that you have lost Momplaisir,*

See, here is his hide upon my back,
Upon my back, my back, my back.
Rum tum, tum, rum tum tum,
Here is his skin upon my back."

And he capered around and around.

Everyone froze in his shadow. There were murmurs of "Silence! Listen!" Some were tipsy and believed they had understood wrongly; others, curious and suspicious, crept closer.

The King, surmising the worst, stood up and en-

couraged the singer. "Ah, what a lovely song! Sing it once again."

Bouki, flattered, rendered an encore at the top of his lungs. The guests made bold to finger the jacket.

A cry arose, repeated by all, "King, King, it is indeed the hide of Momplaisir, the hide of your beloved kid!" The guards, dancing about Bouki, rushed forward, raising their *batons.*

"The hide of Momp . . ." began Bouki in astonishment, but he got no further. A blow on his head closed his mouth.

He did not open it again, for Malice jumped up and exhorted the guards, "Gag him, do not let him speak, he will disappear!"

When the beating ended, Bouki was a sorry, misshapen lump. Malice received the reward and became the King's counselor.

From Haiti
Bastien, Rémy. *Anthologie du Folklore Haitien*

TALES OF MAGIC

Greedy Mariani

On a high road, far from any village, lived Mariani. Alone. And little wonder. Mariani was a woman, the possessor of a quick temper, a scolding tongue, a greedy disposition, a. . . . But you will see.

Travelers on the high road, surprised by nightfall, would approach Mariani's hut with thankfulness. "If you could spare but a crumb of hospitality. . . ." they would beg.

And a crumb was what they received. No more, no less. A mere corner of the hut in which to curl up. No bed. No blanket. A pillow? Ha, ha, a good jest, that. As for food, a bean, a grain or two of rice—and this only if

Mariani were in an unaccountably good humor. Which happened, oh, once in ten years.

To bring her entertainment to a proper close, Mariani would awaken her guests at dawn. Equipped with two hefty arms, she would strip them of their valuables and drive them on their way. At least they had an early start on the day's journey. But were they grateful for that? Indeed not. Away they stumbled, shaking their fists, shrieking bad words. "Miser! Witch! Thief!" But probably true. Very likely true.

One stormy night Mariani was occupied pouring cane-sugar syrup into a huge cauldron. A knock at the door. *"Honneur."*

"Respect," replied Mariani, and opened the door.

A man stood there eying the doorsill. Timidly he requested shelter to await the end of the tempest. As the lizard greets the ant, so Mariani welcomed the traveler.

This one turned back into the rain and wind, then returned with a sack stuffed to its mouth. He let it fall to the floor with a clink. No doubt about it. Only silver clinks so clinkily. Mariani watched with interest.

The man politely excused himself, backed out the door. Again he came, bearing a second bag. This one also clinked. Back and forth he went, twice more; each time returning with another sack. All stuffed as plumply as a roasted turkey. All clinking beautifully.

Mariani, missing not a clink, set the cauldron over the fire. She busied herself shelling peanuts for the making of cane-syrup *tablettes,* all the while dreaming of those sacks of silver, which would, if she had her way, soon be stashed away under the *mapou* tree in her garden.

Soon the rain ended. A star appeared. The man raised himself from the bench and prepared to load his mules. He did not forget to thank his hostess with much courtesy. But thanks are a matter of nothing to a miser, a witch, a thief.

"Not so fast, my dear sir," spoke Mariani. "Are these then your manners? You shield yourself from the rain under my roof. Now you think to leave without paying me a *centime*. Shame!"

The traveler, his head bowed, murmured pardons. *"Non,* but *non,* madame, I thought to leave you in return for your gracious hospitality"—(he must have been joking) —"a sack of silver. If you yourself would care to choose one bag from the four. . . ."

"One from the four? All four of the four! Is it my fault that my lodging costs so dear? To be exact, four sacks of silver. And fortunate you are that the price is not five or six sacks. The idea! Only one bag of silver for an entire hour's shelter. Actually, closer to an hour and a quarter. . . ."

The stranger did not reply (clever stranger). He loaded

the mules with three bags of silver. Not an easy thing to do in the black dark. Then he urged the beasts before him with the tune of his snapping whip:

> *Kalinda, ding ding ding daou,*
> *Kalinda, ding ding ding daou,*
> *Kalinda, ding ding ding daou,*
> *Kalinda, ding ding ding ding daou.*

Mariani stood on her doorstep and cried, "Thief! Render me my due!"

The stranger seemed not to hear. Maybe he was deaf, which at the moment would have been a blessing. He flicked the mules with the singing whip.

Mariani ran after him, tossing insults and abuse with a free tongue. No response. The man stared at the ground as if in deep thought. Thus they journeyed for some time, the mules and the man mute, Mariani railing and ranting.

Finally, having screeched herself out of breath, the old woman panted, "Monsieur, the syrup boils, the syrup boils, I must prepare my *tablettes*. Give me my money!"

Sang the stranger,

> *"Mariani, I begin to hear you now.*
> *Better to turn back now,*
> *Poor Mariani."*

He flipped his whip, and in their sacks the silver tinkled a tune:

Kalinda, ding ding ding daou,
Kalinda, ding ding ding daou,
Kalinda, ding ding ding daou,
Kalinda, ding ding ding ding daou.

"I mock your counsel! Counsel I wish not. I wish my money!" howled Mariani. Still she followed the little band, the mules and the man.

For a long time, a long, long time they marched. In silence. In darkness. Along the long lonely road without encountering a soul. Not one soul.

Weary and out of patience, Mariani threatened, "Thief, I will escort you to the judge. You shall not escape me. Certain it is that my syrup scorches to cinders. You shall pay me for that as well as for lodging."

The driver-of-mules repeated his song,

> *"Mariani, I hear you now, I hear you now.*
> *Better to turn back, turn back,*
> *Poor Mariani."*

But Mariani, along with a quick temper, scolding tongue and greedy disposition, possessed a stubborn nature. Return home while three bags of silver clinked just beyond her fingers? An absurdity. They continued the journey. On and on.

At last, as they approached a village, dawn announced itself. A cock crowed.

Greedy Mariani

The mules vanished. The man faced about and gazed directly at Mariani. *Hélas!* What did she see?

A skull with empty sockets. Bared teeth. Bones clinking, clinking, clinking in the wind.

Mariani fell, stone dead of shock. And the zombi—for so he was—disappeared among the tombs of a nearby cemetery.

From Haiti
Bastien, Rémy. *Anthologie du Folklore Haitien*

The Three Fairies

There was once a widow who had a very pretty, kind and good daughter. Being sickly, the woman worried much about dying and leaving her daughter alone in the world. Every night she prayed that the girl would find a good husband who would care for and protect her.

The girl was indeed virtuous and industrious. But not flirtatious at all. Nor yet coy. Nor coquettish. So the young men of the town, being more jocund than judicious, avoided her.

There was in that place a wealthy *señor* who was looking for a girl to marry. A hardworking girl. A comely girl. A good girl. Well, you say, so there's the story. The

señor married the widow's daughter, and that was that.
Nooooo . . . there were complications, and that was *not*
that. At least not right away.

True, the *señor* did come to visit the widow. True, he
admired the daughter greatly—and said so. True, the
widow was most encouraging, pointing out her daughter's attractions: her quietness, her diligence, her tender-
ness, her flawless complexion, her honey-hued hair, the
beauty mark on her chin, and on and on.

"But," inquired the *señor,* who had been pondering,
"can she spin? Can she sew? Can she embroider? For in
my business there is much of cotton and silk."

"Por supuesto, naturally she can sew, spin and embroider to a fare-thee-well. There is nothing that girl cannot do. She spins a thread as fine as a spider's. Her stitches
are smaller than the footprints of a fly. She can embroider
a bird so you reach to stroke its feathers."

"In that case," announced the *señor,* "it is settled. If she
is *that* good a spinner, a sewer, an embroiderer, I will
marry her. I shall arrange at once for the wedding." And
away he went.

The widow was overjoyed. You would have thought
she was the one getting married. And what did the
daughter have to say? (Though it was by now rather
late for her to say anything, even about her own mar-
riage.)

"Mama, I heard what you said. How could you be so

foolish? I know little of sewing, nothing of embroidery, and less of spinning. What will that *señor* think of me when we are married?"

"You are the foolish one, daughter. Surely there is a solution to the problem. All you have to do is think of it. I did this for your good, you well know."

When she went to bed that night the poor girl wept a thousand or more tears thinking of the terrible lies her mother had told. Not to speak of what might befall *her* for having deceived the *señor*. She had just resolved to go to him early the next day and confess the truth about herself when she heard a slight noise. Sitting up, she saw three strangers. On top of everything else! The poor girl wept harder than ever.

However, the strangers assured her they were fairies and had come to help her. Their only condition, they said, would be an invitation to her wedding. The girl was only too happy to consent, saying they could come as her dearest relatives. They disappeared, and the girl fell asleep.

Days passed and preparations were made for the wedding. The girl informed her *novio* that she had invited a few of her cousins whom she loved very much to come to the wedding feast.

The day of the celebration arrived, passed and died away. That night all the wedding guests sat down at the table for dinner. Three chairs remained vacant.

"For whom are these reserved?" asked the groom.

At that moment came a knock at the door. It opened and three old horrors entered whom the girl introduced as her cousins.

Dinner was served, and the whole world was content and ate tremendously. When it was over the husband arose and went to speak to the girl's kin, who were now his cousins as well as his wife's.

He asked the first, "Hear me, cousin. Will you tell me why you are so humped and one-eyed?" (A blunt man, the bridegroom.)

"Ay, my son! From all the embroidery I did in my life."

The husband whispered to his wife, "From now on I forbid you to embroider. I can pay to have this done and I do not wish you to be so deformed as your unlucky cousin."

Then he asked the second, "And why is it your two arms are so unequal?"

"Because I have spent my whole life spinning."

The *señor* took his wife's hand. "Nevermore will you spin, my love."

And finally he questioned the third of the cousins. "What is the matter with your eyes, that they burst from your head as grapes from their skins?"

"Ah, so would yours if your life had been spent sewing and reviewing tiny stitches."

"This, my dear, shall not happen to you," said the *señor,* turning to his wife. "You are to do no more sewing. None at all."

The very next day the husband gathered up all his wife's sewing equipment and hurled it out the door, since he cared more for his wife's beauty than all the work she could do. The two lived most happily and the girl never had to grieve herself to explain away the lies her poor mother had told.

From Puerto Rico
Ramírez de Arellano, Rafael. *Folklore Portorriqueño*

TALES OF PEOPLE

Juan Bobo

There was once a boy called Juan Bobo. Juan Bobo—what kind of name is that? Why, the name for one who is idle, thickheaded and a simpleton. For so Juan Bobo was.

One day his mother sent him to town to buy three things: meat, cane syrup and needles. "One, two, three, Juan Bobo. Do not forget."

Juan Bobo harnessed the mare with saddle baskets and set off for the village. First he bought the syrup and poured it into the baskets. Then the meat and needles were slung in on top of the syrup.

Home trudged Juan Bobo. The syrup-coated meat accompanied him, but not the syrup or the needles. They were left behind, where they had fallen or dribbled through the mesh of the baskets. The syrup also disappeared into the dozens of flies that buzzed about the boy and the horse.

When Juan Bobo arrived home it took no brilliance to realize how stupid he had been. His mother beat him, crying, "Animal! No better are you than an animal! How can you pour syrup into a basket and expect it to stay there? And the needles! Naturally they made their escape through the holes. How is it possible for you to be so simple? Truly you are good for naught!"

"Mama, do not distract yourself," said Juan Bobo. "The syrup was eaten by the *señoritas* of the dark mantles. Tomorrow I shall denounce them as thieves before the judge."

"*Ay,* Juan," sighed his mother. "You are more foolish than fools. Had I not needed you, I should long since have tossed you out of this world. You serve for nothing. In fact, you are only a burden to me."

"Mama, disturb yourself not. Tomorrow I go without fail to denounce the *señoritas,* those young ladies of the dark mantles."

"Well, well, boy, leave tomorrow's work for the morrow. But go *now* to the *comae* to borrow her three-legged pot that I may make a stew of the meat. And hurry. I have no more time to fritter away." This was a hint to Juan Bobo, but of course he did not heed it.

Strolling and straggling, he managed with great luck to stray into his godmother's house and there ask for the loan of the pot. That turned out to be a kettle of the sort used long ago, of iron, with three legs and as large as a washtub.

Juan grabbed up the pot—it took all his muscle—and started away. After ten minutes on the dusty road he dropped the pot to wipe his dripping face. Then he addressed the pot so: "Look, already I am worn out from holding you! With three legs you are better able to walk than I. Go ahead. March now, hep, one, two, three. I will follow you."

When the pot remained glued to the same spot Juan Bobo asked, "What's wrong with you? Is it that you do not know the way? Then I shall lead and you will go behind."

Still the pot refused to budge.

"Slothful, that is what you are. Lazy and slothful. Too lazy to walk. So you desire to be carried. A pretty thing that is, that I, with only two legs, must support you who have three. No, *señor,* it behooves you to walk. Walk you must and walk you *will.*"

To Juan's disgust, the pot moved not one of its three feet—not a wiggle. With a club he carried, the boy

whacked the pot furiously and punched it besides. "Walk, walk, slothful one. Advance, Mama is waiting for us!"

Thus the two made their way, Juan using his feet both to transport himself and to shove the pot. On reaching a place where the road divided itself into two little paths, the boy seized the pot and set it firmly on one of the trails.

"Listen, you. Here is the track running straight before you. Not even an idiot could lose it. Now follow it as fast as you can. I shall take the other path. We'll see who arrives at my house first, you or I—and the winner gets a lick of cane syrup."

Juan Bobo dashed to the other trail and set his fingers to the ground. "Ready?" he cried. "At the one, at the two, at the three!" And away he sped, swift as a wheel rolling downhill.

Out of breath, he reached his home. "Mama! Mama! Has it come? Did it beat me?"

"Boy, has *what* come?"

"The pot, Mama, the pot. We raced to see which would win."

"Juan Bobo, I could kill you. This moment I could kill you. What a brainless one you are. Go, go at once to bring me the pot!" screamed the mother in a fury.

Juan Bobo, also in a fury but in a flutter as well, climbed the hill till he found the pot, still and stubborn as a stone. Juan took his revenge by casting against the pot all the indignities his mother had called him.

"You see, laziness? You have no consideration. Through your fault Mama was about to smack me. Indeed she *will* smack me if we don't return soon. You should be ashamed, you with three feet and I with only two and yet *I* arrived first." And he delivered two good kicks to the pot.

As the path began to slope at that point, the pot started slowly to roll downhill. "So at last you are running?" asked Juan. "I have frightened you at last? About time." With satisfaction he followed the pot home.

Early the next day Juan Bobo, true to his promise, went to speak with the judge.

"*Señor juez,*" he said, "I come to denounce the *señoritas* of the dark mantles for eating up our syrup."

"*Señoritas?* I see no *señoritas. What señoritas?*" asked the judge severely.

"These, the same that you see here," answered Juan and pointed out some flies stuck to the wall.

"Ah! The *señoritas* of the black mantles. Flies, you wish to say?"

"That exactly. They stole my syrup. Either they pay me or you must punish them."

"Juan, listen to what you must do," spoke the judge, with a solemn face and a body heaving with laughter. "Wherever you see one of these *señoritas* take the club that you carry, strike her and kill her. Simple enough, no?"

"Very well, *señor* judge." And at that very instant, *tras!* he aimed a tremendous blow at the head of the hapless judge—a *señorita* of the dark mantle had alighted on the man's bald head. A good aim. A fair hit. A *very* fair hit. Unfortunately.

Juan Bobo was sent to prison. Not even there was he left in peace by the teasing little *señoritas* of the dark mantles. Only his mother, poor soul, was granted for a time a measure of tranquillity.

From Puerto Rico
Ramírez de Arellano, Rafael. *Folklore Portorriqueño*

The Shepherd
and the Princess

There was once and twice make thrice a King so hardheaded and vain that he wanted everything done completely to his taste. Not to anyone else's. For what did anyone else matter? *He* was the King. Only *he* was *important*.

This King had a daughter—a beautiful daughter, too, which was more than he deserved. Many were the princes who fell in love with her. However, so disagreeable was the King that the princes hesitated to brave him, even to request the princess' hand.

It happened that through the fields surrounding the palace a young shepherd often wandered. He was a good boy, beloved by all the peasants for his many kindnesses. To no one's amazement, this shepherd was also in love with the princess. But then, who wasn't? Having more sense than most, he realized he was in no position to woo her. Even the most amiable of kings balk at shepherds for sons-in-law. So he went about his work singing—ballads, ditties, arias, lyrics—and of course, love songs. The princess found his voice enchanting—and his person as well, for he was a fine-looking fellow.

Some time went by and the King decided it was time to find a husband for his daughter. Being as unstraightforward (or could we say crooked-forward?) as he was, he spent days thinking up a strange and exotic task for the would-be husband.

He thought of it all right. The suitor must bring him three things. And what were these three things? A glass filled with all the waters from everywhere; a bouquet of every blossom blooming; and a handful of hazelnuts of *ay . . . ay . . . ay!*

Princes came from far and wide, attracted by the beauty of the princess. But on learning the conditions of the task they sadly returned to their lands. After all, everywhere is enormous; every flower is a great many; and where on earth is *ay . . . ay . . . ay?* An impossible exercise the King had set. Ab–so–lute–ly impossible.

Only the shepherd, hearing the order of the King, decided to leave his sheep and go in search of every water, a nosegay of each flower, and a fistful of filberts of *ay . . . ay . . . ay!* Humming a tune, he set out, walking and walking and walking and walking—oh, say maybe a hundred walkings more, until he came to a field with a hut in it, and in the hut a light.

Toc, toc, toc, knocked the shepherd at the door to seek shelter for the night. As no one answered, he opened the door and entered. He passed through the house, seeing no one. At last, in the kitchen he found an idiot watching a pot set over the fire and laughing.

"What are you doing?" asked the shepherd.

"Taking out those that have come and waiting for those that are about to come," answered the idiot. And sure enough, he was scooping out the beans that floated on the water and awaiting those that would rise from the bottom of the pot.

"And you, have you no parents?"

"Oh, yes," replied the idiot, "but they are looking for yesterday's dinner."

So they were, since they were searching the fields for blobs of wool that the sheep had left hung on the brambles. These they expected to sell and with the money pay for the dinner of the previous day.

The shepherd fell to musing. Perhaps this idiot with his clever ideas could help him with his search. The first thing to do was ask. This he did. And the idiot advised him as to how to find the three items.

On went the shepherd, once more walking and walking and walking and . . . but enough; we've been through that before. After a good deal more walking the shepherd found himself back at court. At once he informed the King that he had obtained the three things and was ready to exchange them for the hand of the princess.

When the princess learned of the shepherd's return she was overjoyed. With a bit more thought she grew oversaddened. What if the shepherd were mistaken? What if even one of the three articles was lacking? Her father would pause not a moment to summon the executioner.

When the shepherd bowed before the King, this one asked, "It is certain you have found what I asked for?"

"Indeed, sir. I have them with me."

"*Bueno,* give me the first."

The shepherd handed him a glass of water. "This glass holds all the waters, since it is water from the sea, where flow the waters from rain, from springs, from rivers, from streams, from fountains."

"Very well," said the King. "You have brought me the first. Let me view the second. Where is it?"

"Take it, sir." A honeycomb was popped into the King's hand. "This is the bouquet of every blossom blooming; to make it, the bees had to gather honey from all the flowers."

"Good enough, good enough, but now let us go on to

the last article."

"The hazelnuts of *ay . . . ay . . . ay?* I have them in this basket, sir. Have the goodness to extract them."

The King reached in, but no sooner had his hand touched the bottom of the basket than he began to dance up and down and cry, "*Ay . . . ay . . . ay!*"

In the basket, along with the hazelnuts, the shepherd had placed some small crabs that eagerly nipped the monarch's fingers. Served him right. Still, the old rascal kept to his bargain; for the price of a glass of water, a piece of honeycomb, a potpourri of nuts and crabs, he bestowed his daughter on the shepherd.

The princess was so content with the shepherd's triumph she jumped for joy. The wedding was arranged. The two were married and lived happily for years and years and years.

From Puerto Rico
Ramírez de Arellano, Rafael. *Folklore. Portorriqueño*

The Miser Who
Received His Due

There once was a miser so miserly that for a few
silver coins he was capable of tossing his soul to the
Devil. Greediness is bad enough. But worse still, he was
married to a grasping woman. Worst of all, they had a
daughter more stingy than pretty. Sad. Sad. Not for
them. Just for those having to deal with them. Such as
slaves.

With his slaves this miser enjoyed a reputation for
cruelty and injustice. They hated him for the beatings
he handed out. And he was forever handing *those* out—
ummm, yes. Liberal with the last he was—a model of

liberality. However, the slaves were unappreciative of his generosity. Didn't even give a thank-you.

One of the slaves, Tito, the most badly treated and amply flogged of the lot, had still enough spirit to wish to repay the master for his bounty of whippings.

"I will make a wager," he told his companion slaves one evening, "that by the use of my wits I will, before a month is out, be seated at my master's table." (Not that that was much of an honor, or pleasure either; the *señora* skimped on food as on everything else.)

"If I do not succeed you may denounce me to the master. And we know what he is apt to do about *that*. But—if I win you will furnish me with a certain amount of money. Enough, added to what I have already saved, to buy my freedom. Done?"

"Done!" cried the others, amused by his audacity.

The next day the master, whip in hand, was inspecting the slaves' work in the fields. Tito neared him and asked in a low, timid and mysterious voice, "My master, sir, could you tell me the value of a bar of gold of such a size?" and he stretched out a finger.

The master, startled, pretended indifference. "Ah, boy," he said, *"valdría mucho.* That would be worth much, much!"

But as soon as he reached his house the miser called his wife and told her what had happened. "So, husband? The slaves have nothing of importance to fix their minds on. They create fancies. . . ."

"Wife, wife, do you not see? He has found gold. Gold not in nuggets or coin—gold in *bars*. He has discovered the place of it. Naturally he knows not the value—and in all innocence has asked me. Ah, if we could find it. A bar of gold the bigness of a finger!" And he sighed and murmured with longing.

After that day the master kept Tito always in view. So closely were his eyes focused on the boy, his blows on the other slaves barely hit the mark. Sometimes they missed completely. Swish! Swish! *"Bueno, hombre, now will you work?"* And all the time he was beating a bush.

Moreover, on every occasion the miser gabbled and joked with Tito in the friendliest way. As if they were both *patrones*.

In a few days the slave sidled up to the miser again. *"Mi amo*, your grace, what would the worth be of a bar of gold, so?" And he tapped his forearm.

The miser's heart nearly stopped. He was convinced that Tito had happened on a cache of gold. Bars the size of an arm! With difficulty he restrained himself from embracing the boy.

"Ah, my fine fellow, such a bar would gain you much silver, a basketful at least." And he slapped Tito on the back in the most jovial manner. They might have been cousins. First cousins. Kissing cousins.

Back at home he was almost too excited to speak. "What did I tell you, wife? That rascal has stumbled on a treasure. Gold bars the size of an arm, an *arm,* wife. And we thought a finger was sizable. *Fantástico.* But yes, they have always told stories of buried treasure hereabouts. And to think Tito was so lucky as to stumble onto it. . . . Wife, I want more respect shown that boy. Not everyone is so intelligent as to recognize a treasure when he sees it. And, daughter, put on your best manners. Your very best. Perhaps you can wheedle the secret from our dear friend. Our dear, dearest friend."

Before long, our dearest friend had been made foreman. Responsibility. Prestige. Confidences. The other slaves, amazed, watched the proceedings silently. They had learned to swallow laughter—what there was of it. From time to time the daughter carried tidbits from the kitchen to Tito. The *señora's* cooking had improved. The smell of gold improves many things.

For a week or so Tito enjoyed his happy state without further mention of gold. Those days were filled with impatience and anxiety for the miser and his wife.

At last the fellow approached slyly once more and asked, "My master, I must ask your grace, how much silver would three such bars bring?" And he patted his leg.

The miser, hysterical with astonishment and joy, cried,

"My dear, dear boy, that would bring enough money to take care of you for the rest of your life!"

Then clapping him on the back—as if Tito were his twin brother no less—the miser put his arm about his shoulder and invited him to eat with them. Tito accepted eagerly.

The dinner was the best that table had ever held. Chicken baked with peppers. Buttered yams. Beans the size of eggs. *Pudín de coco. Café con ron.* A feast. At the table Tito ate the most and best of all that was served. Outside the window clustered slaves—all howling with glee. Soundless glee.

Dinner over, the master signaled his daughter to play the piano. He himself offered Tito a fine cigar. Unable to contain himself any longer, the miser began, "Tito, my son—ha, ha, I call you that as I feel toward you the affection a father feels for his son . . . yes, indeed, my wife and daughter feel the same . . . yes, I assure you, there is something about you. . . . One day perhaps you will be a partner with me. One day soon now, very soon. Perhaps you will even share my humble home. Perhaps (with a sideways glance at his daughter) you may, ha, ha, in time become a part of the family. . . . But meanwhile, Tito, tell me why you have been concerned with the value of gold. With the value of *bars* of gold. . . ."

The slave, having won his bet and within a day or two of gaining his freedom, answered softly, "Ah, my master,

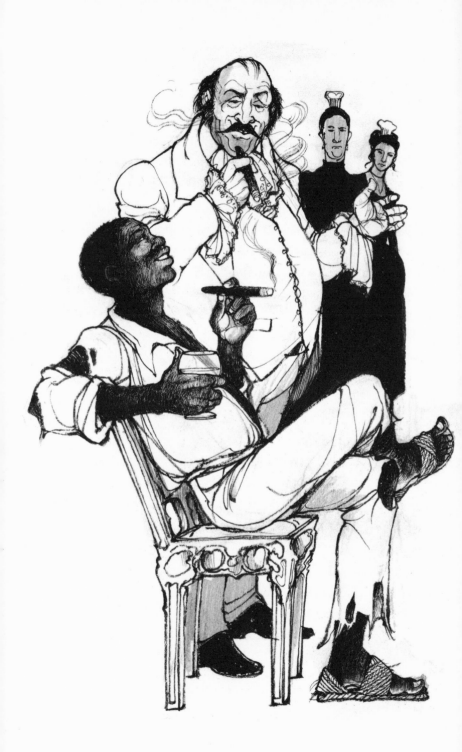

I asked you in case I should ever by chance *come upon* such bars!"

The miser, furious, drove Tito from the house. He commanded the other slaves to beat the boy. But they would not. Not even for the promise of a whipping. And they gladly completed the purse to purchase Tito's freedom.

Naturally the tale spread throughout the region. Everyone knew that for greed the master had spoken of elevating his slave to a partnership. Of taking him into his home. Of even joining him to his family. Until the story became a legend. And the miser became more miserly. But he could never thereafter stifle the hope that someday, somewhere on his land, someone would chance on a treasure of gold bars. . . .

From Cuba
Guirao, Ramón, ed. *Cuentos y Leyendas Negras de Cuba*